EVELYN
and
AVERY

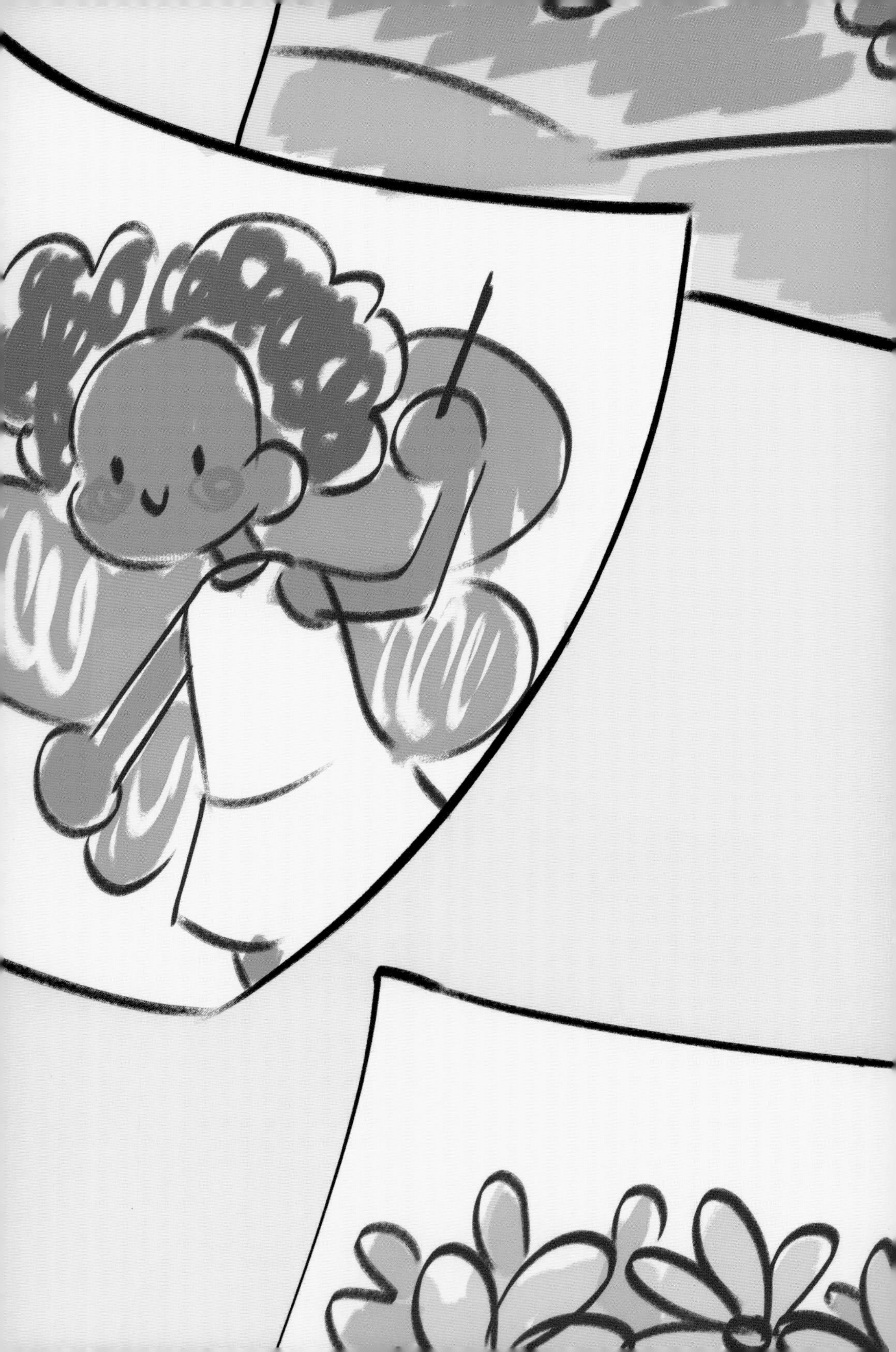

EVELYN and AVERY

The Art of Friendship

by ELLE PIERRE

CLARION BOOKS
Imprints of HarperCollinsPublishers

HARPER
alley

Clarion Books is an imprint of HarperCollins Publishers.
HarperAlley is an imprint of HarperCollins Publishers.

 For information address HarperCollins Children's Books, a division of HarperCollins Publishers, 195 Broadway, New York, NY 10007.
www.harperalley.com

ISBN 978-0-35-868157-1 — ISBN 978-0-35-8681564 (pbk.)

The artist used Clip Studio Paint on their Huion drawing tablet to create the digital illustrations for this book.

24 25 26 27 28 COS 10 9 8 7 6 5 4 3 2 1

First Edition

To Lily

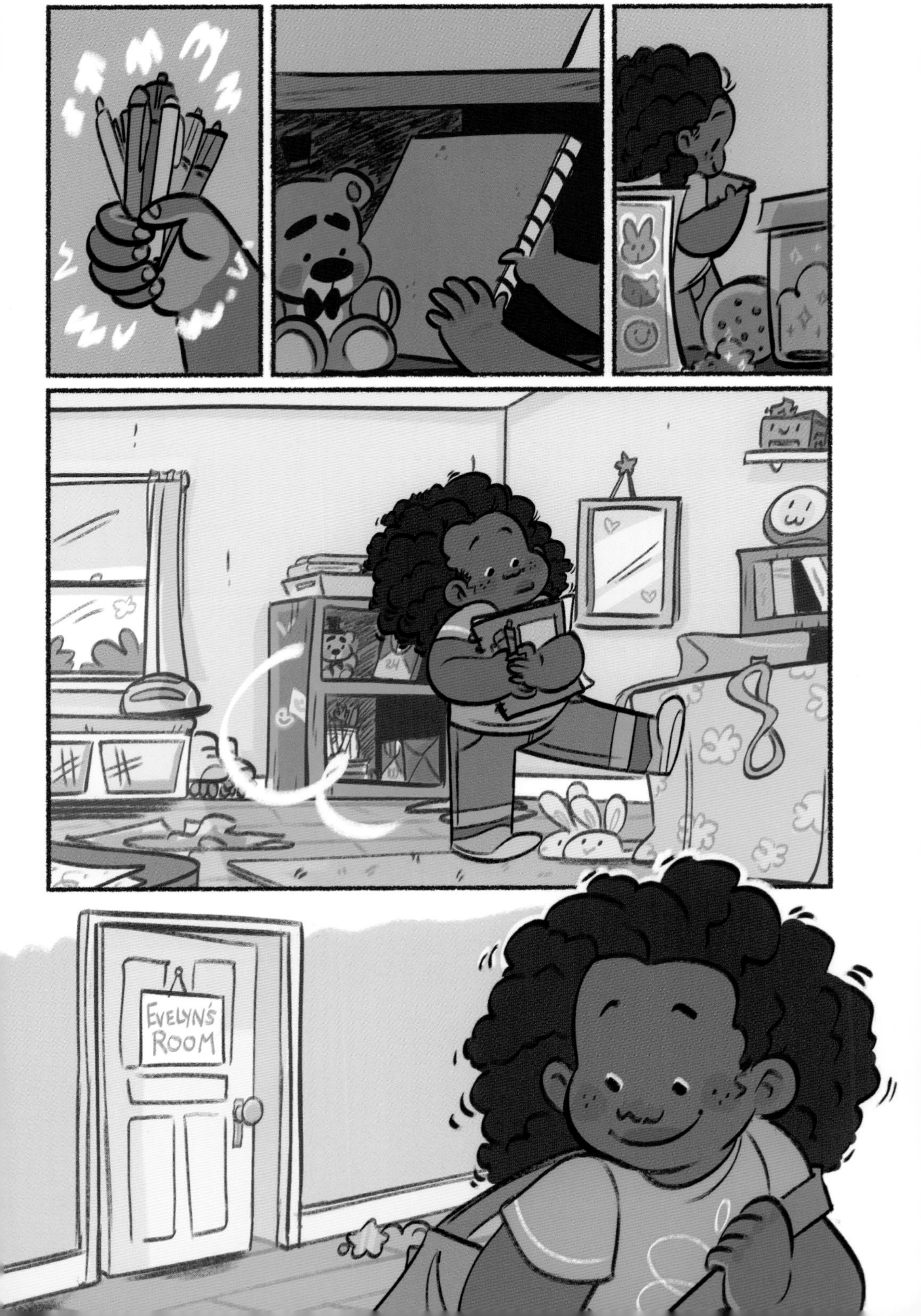
EVELYN'S ROOM

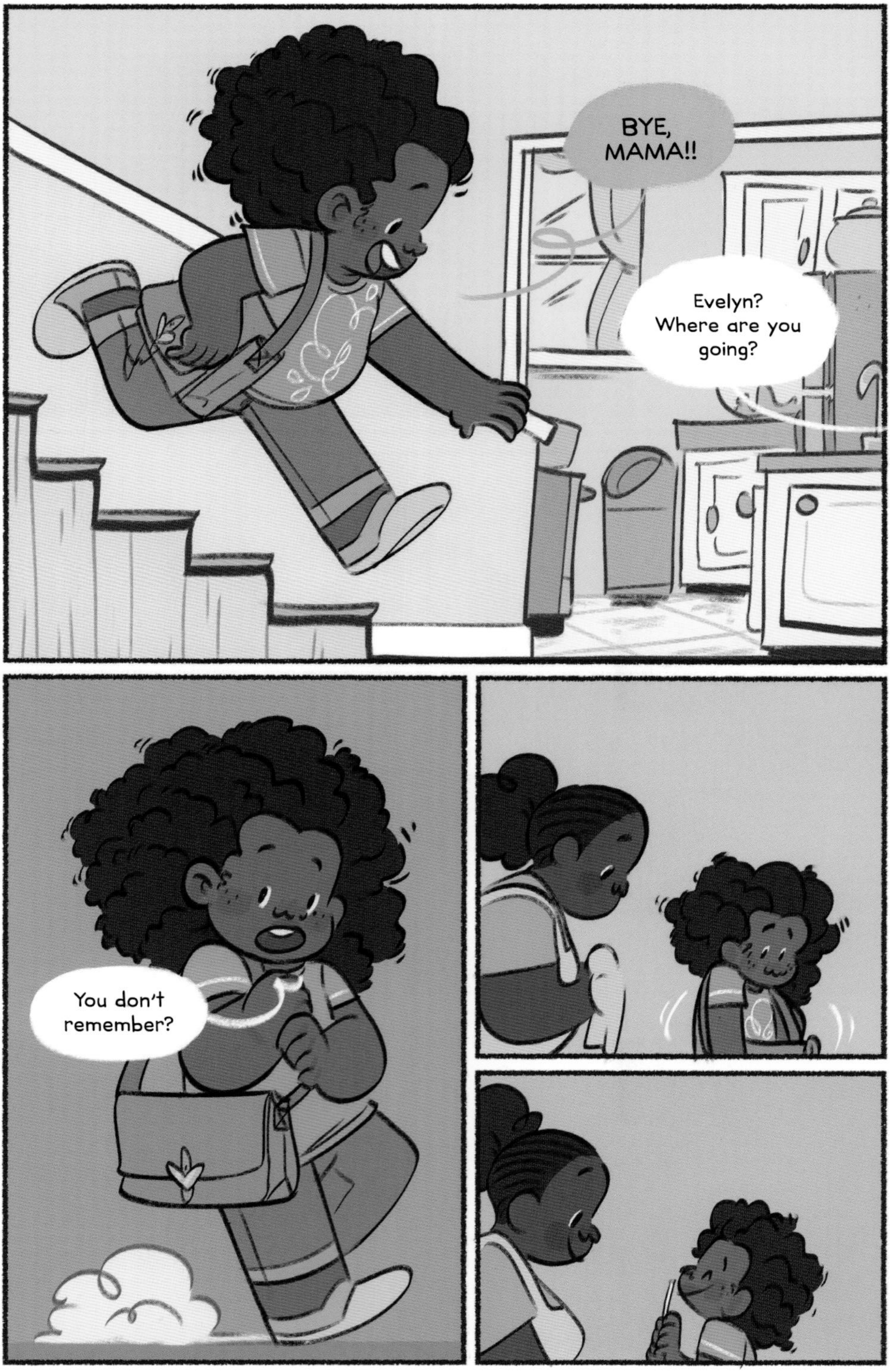

BYE, MAMA!!
Evelyn? Where are you going?
You don't remember?

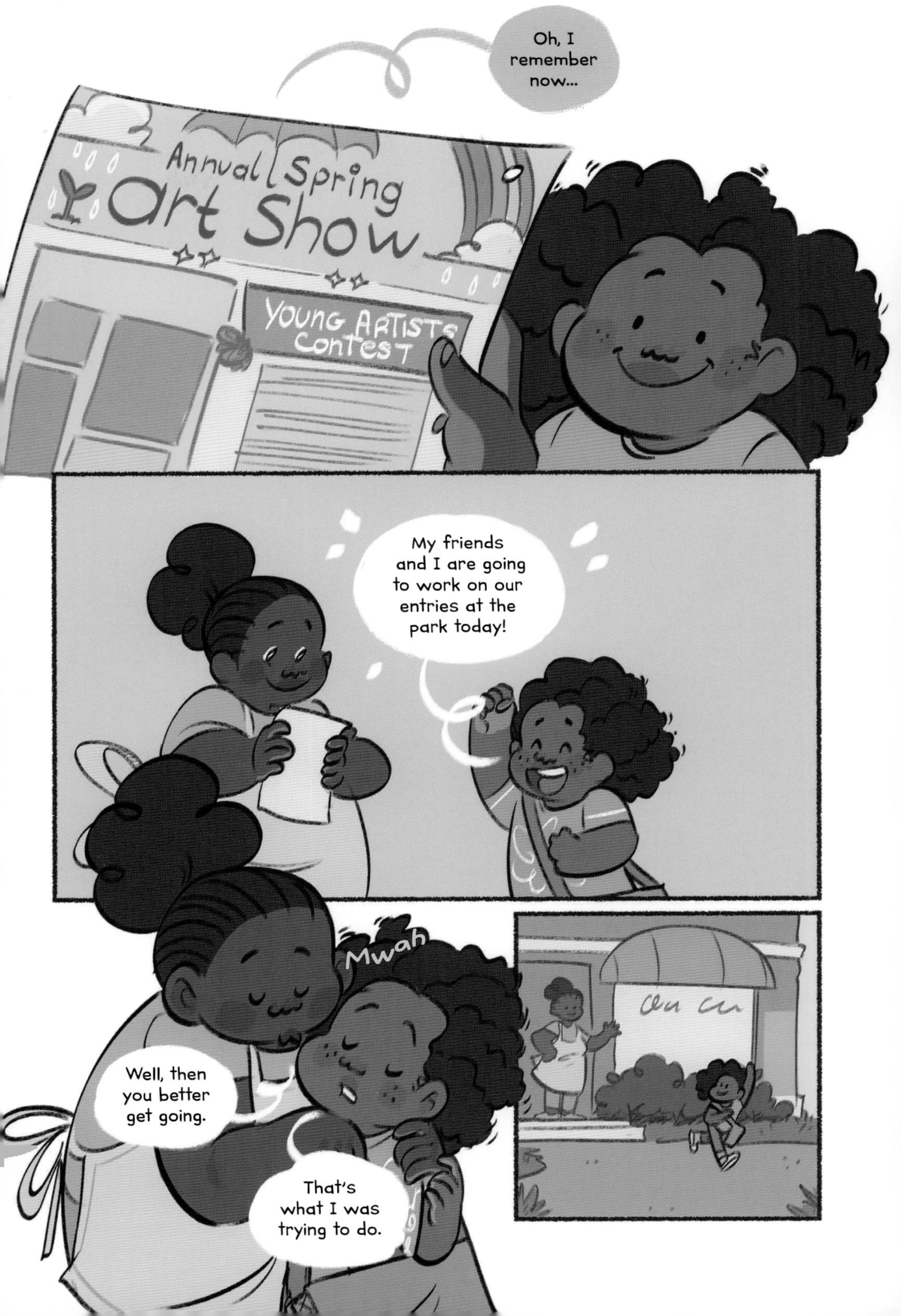
Oh, I remember now...
Annual Spring Art Show
YOUNG ARTISTS CONTEST
My friends and I are going to work on our entries at the park today!
Mwah
Well, then you better get going.
That's what I was trying to do.

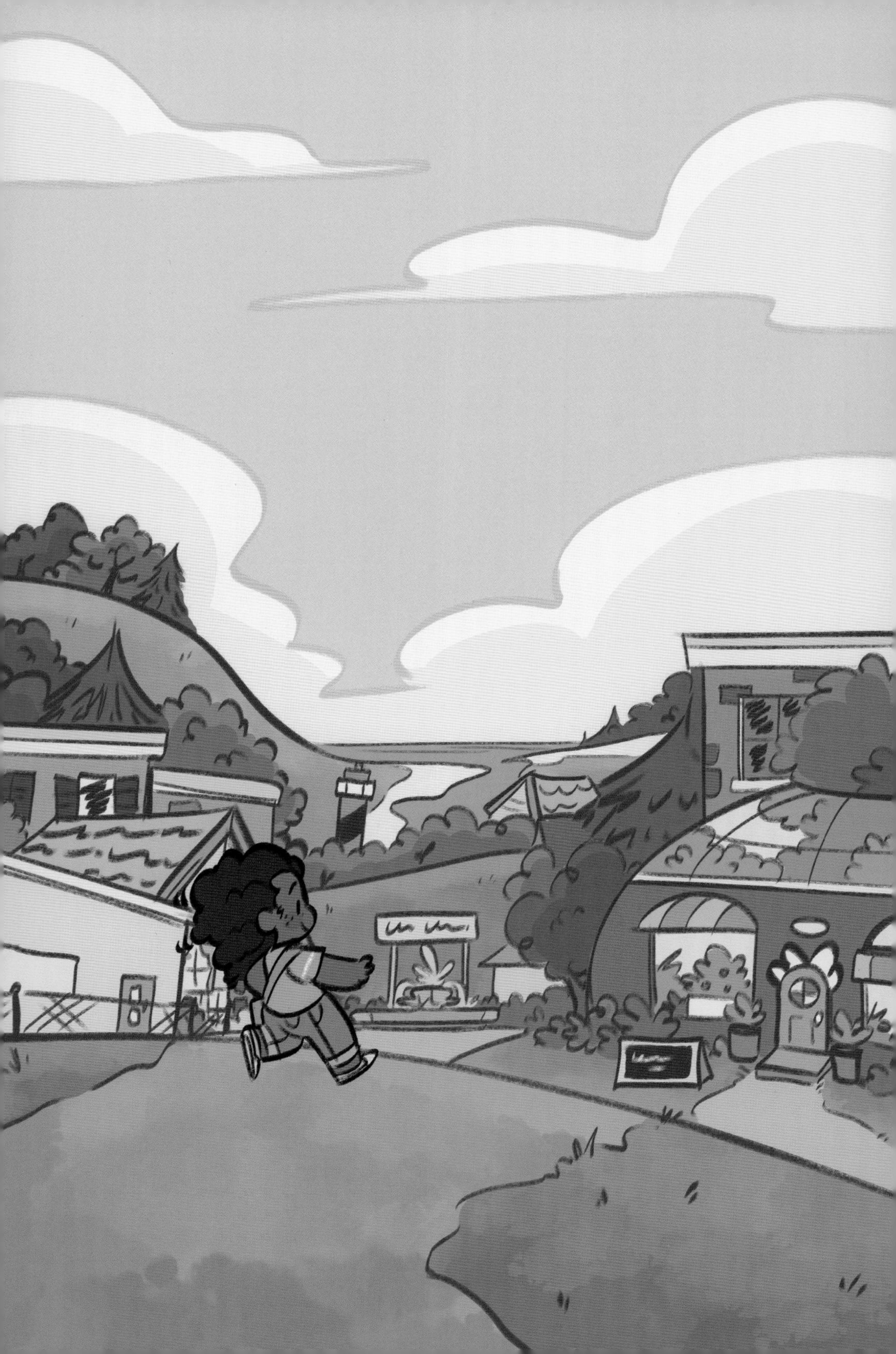

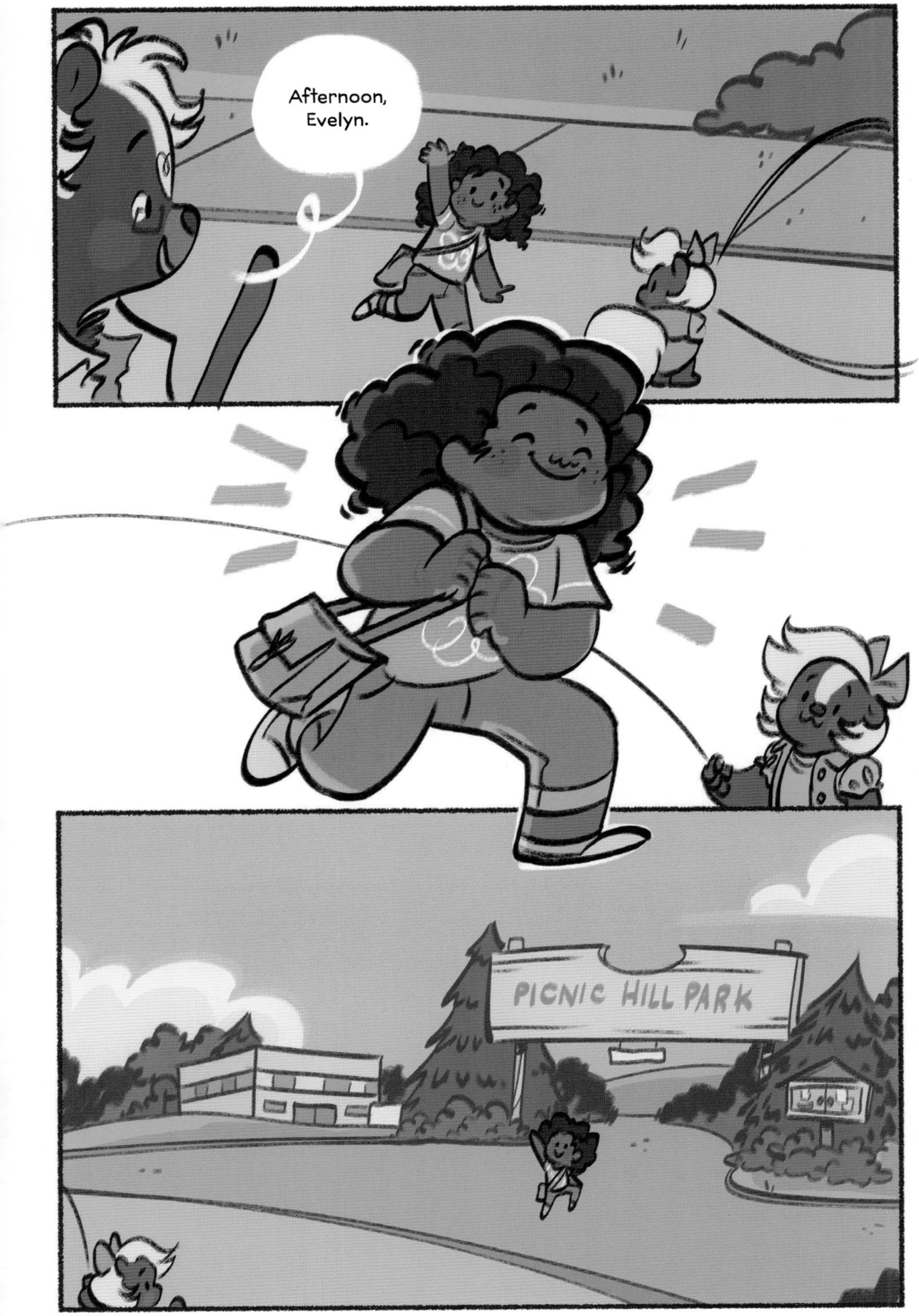
Afternoon, Evelyn.
PICNIC HILL PARK

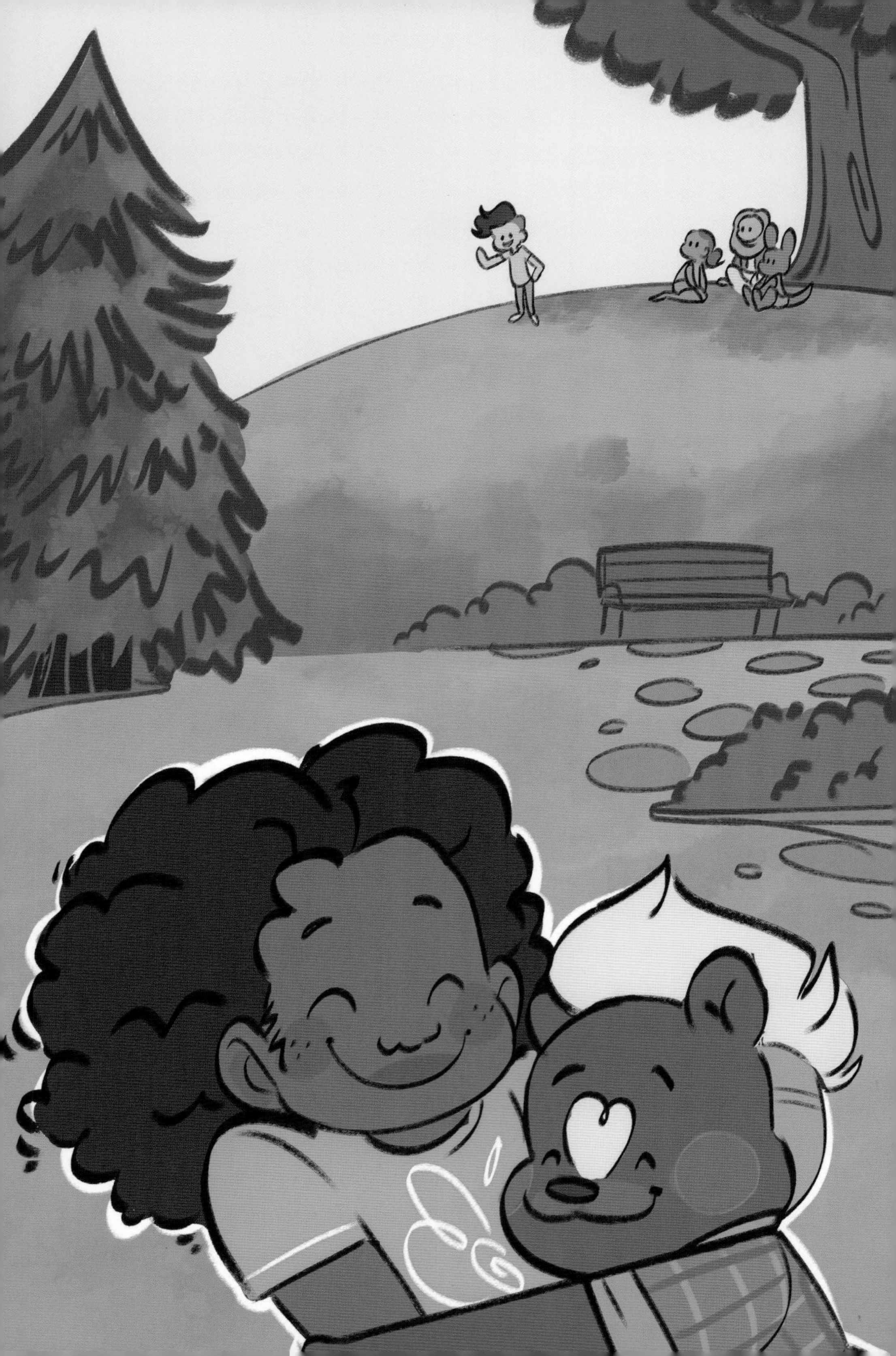

CHAPTER 1

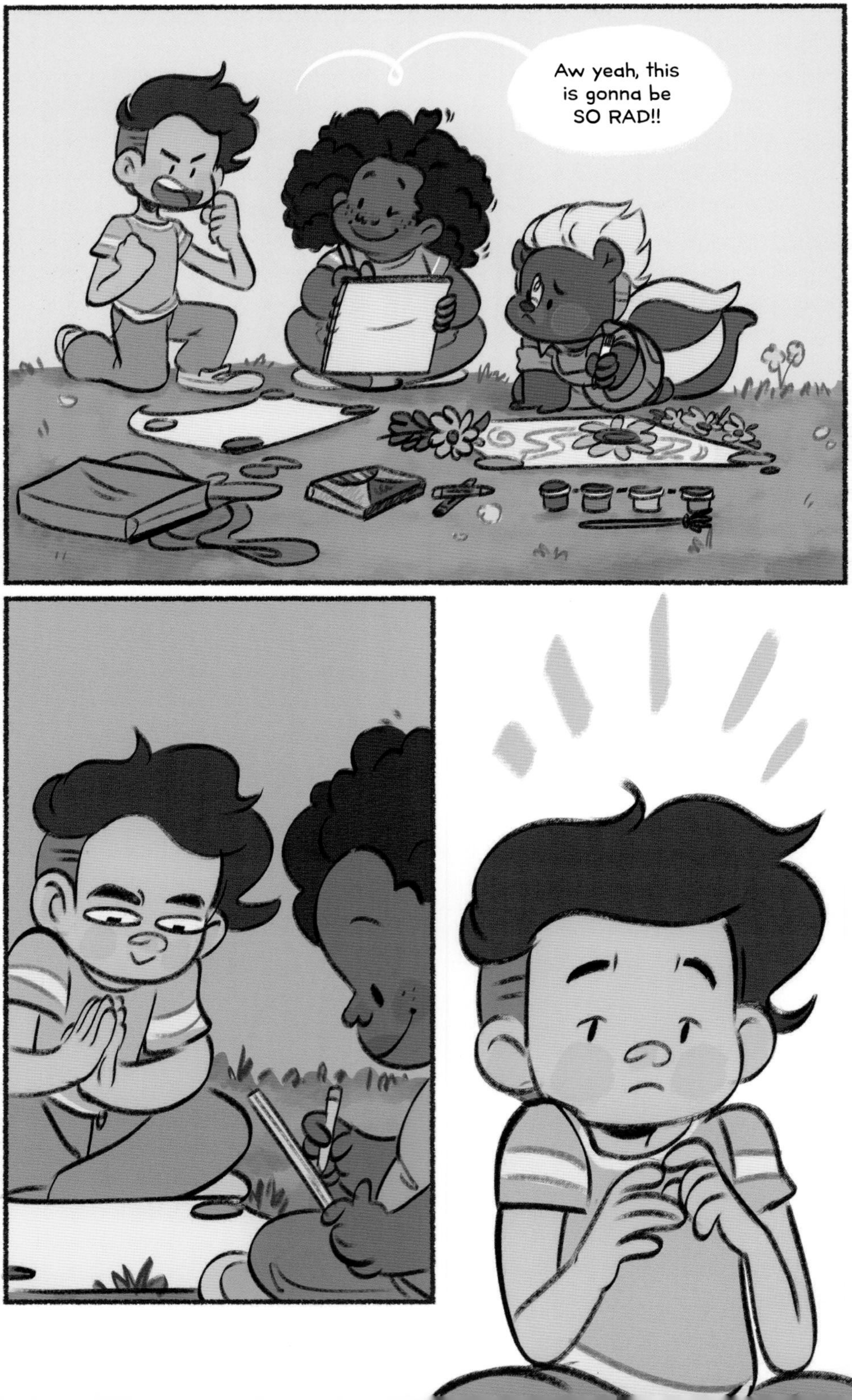
Aw yeah, this
is gonna be
SO RAD!!

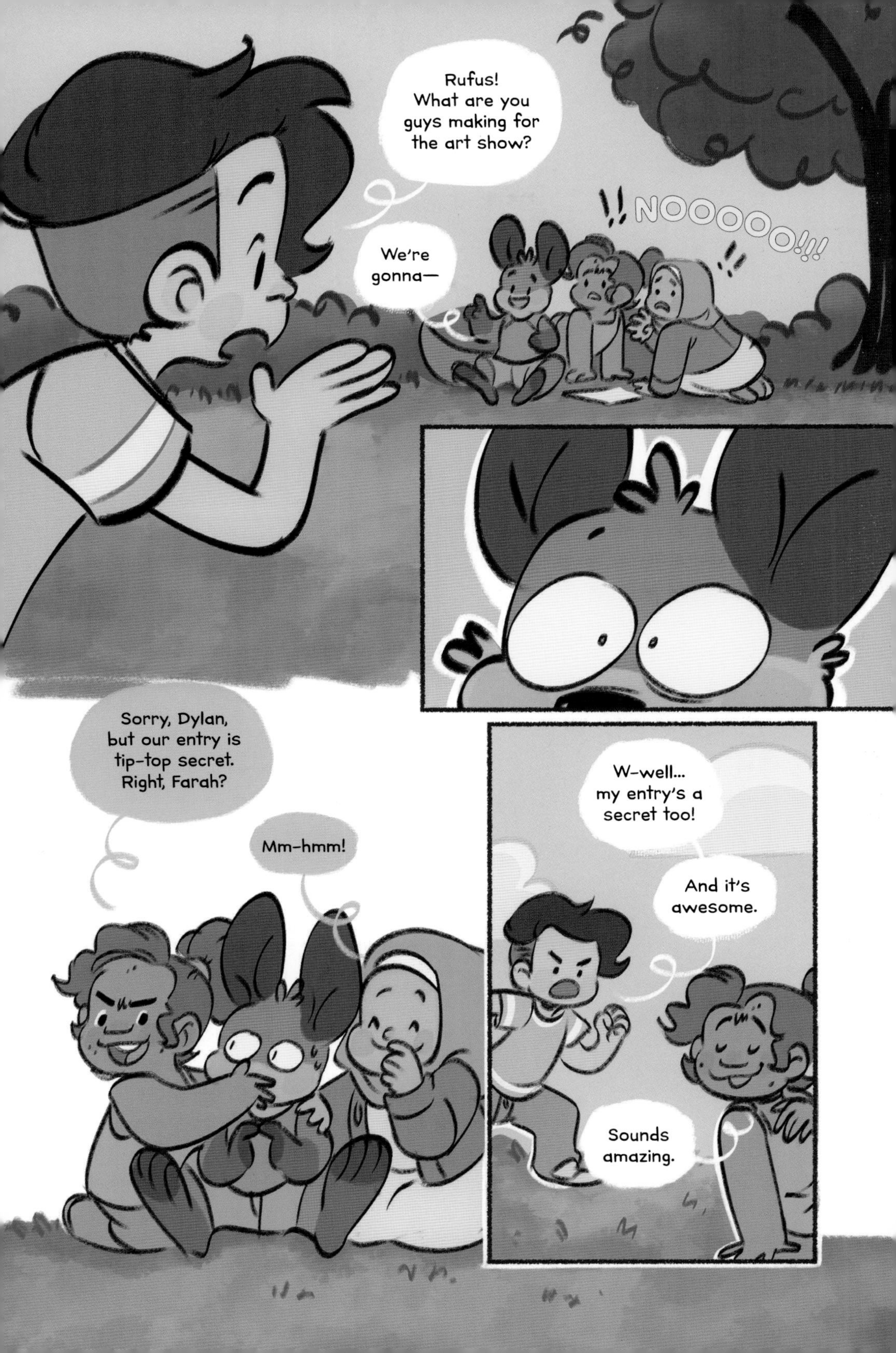
Rufus!
What are you guys making for the art show?
We're gonna—
!! NOOOOO!!!
Sorry, Dylan, but our entry is tip-top secret. Right, Farah?
Mm-hmm!
W-well... my entry's a secret too!
And it's awesome.
Sounds amazing.

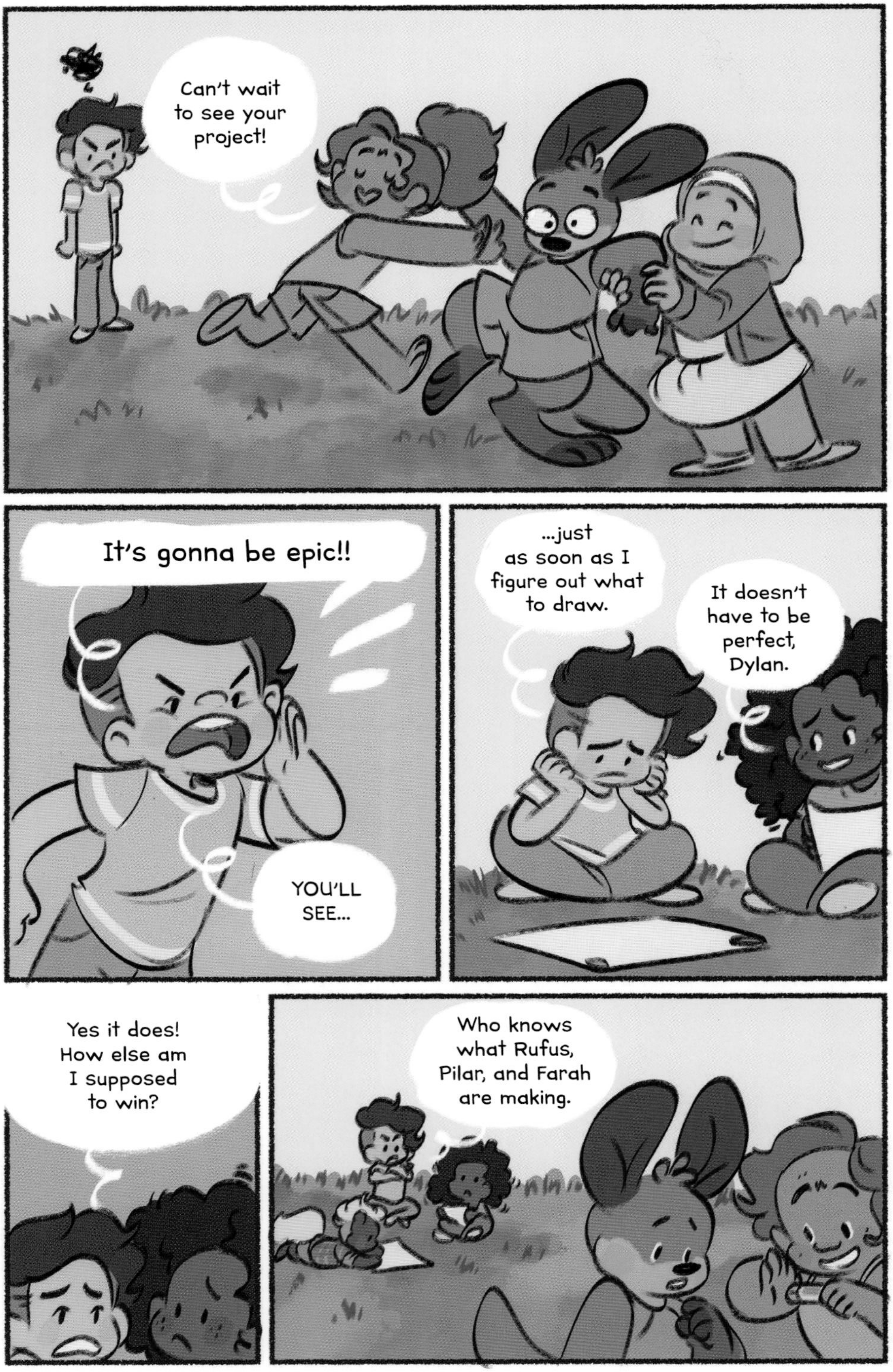

Can't wait to see your project!
It's gonna be epic!!
YOU'LL SEE...
...just as soon as I figure out what to draw.
It doesn't have to be perfect, Dylan.
Yes it does! How else am I supposed to win?
Who knows what Rufus, Pilar, and Farah are making.

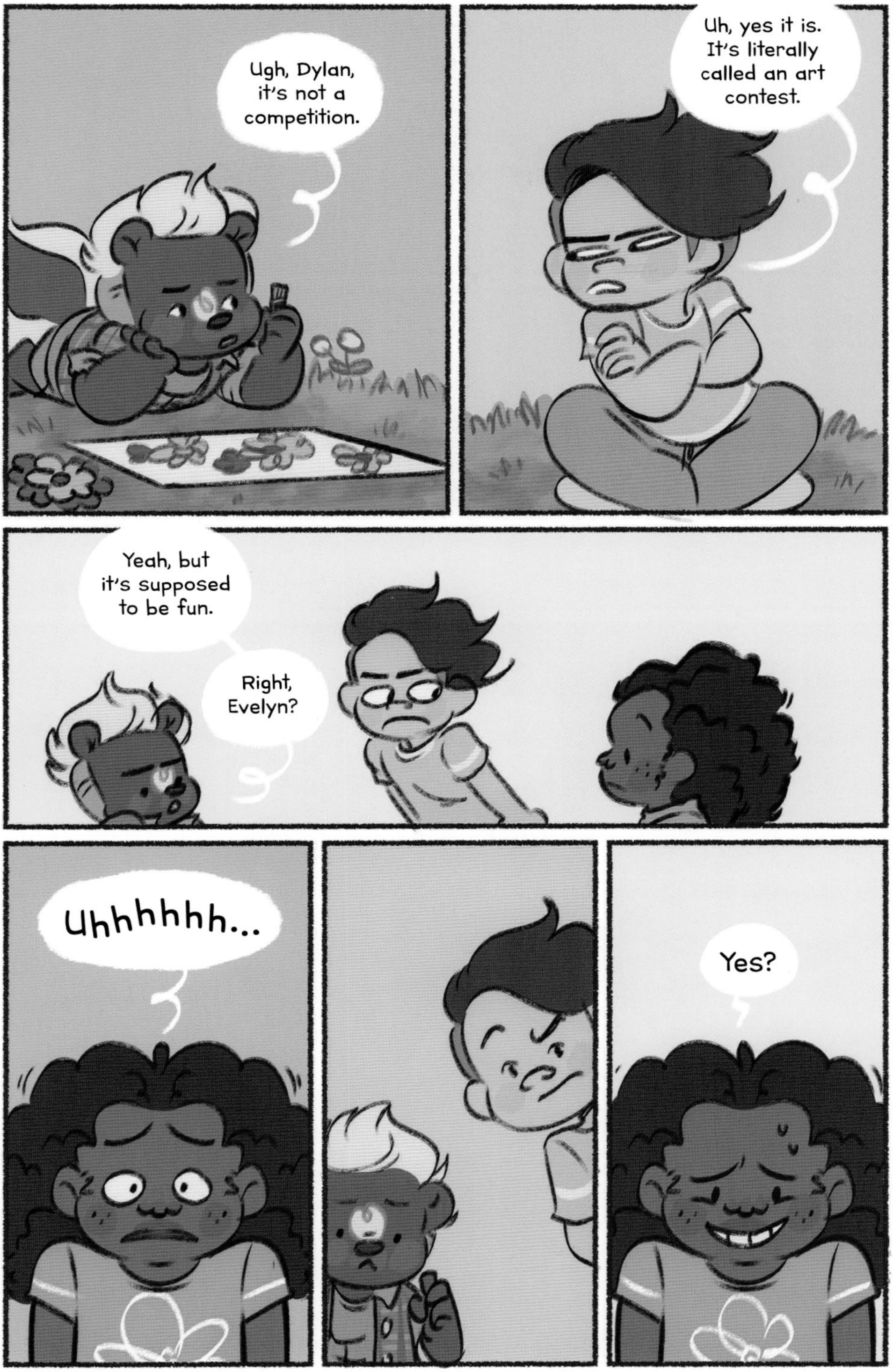
Ugh, Dylan, it's not a competition.
Uh, yes it is. It's literally called an art contest.
Yeah, but it's supposed to be fun.
Right, Evelyn?
Uhhhhhh...
Yes?

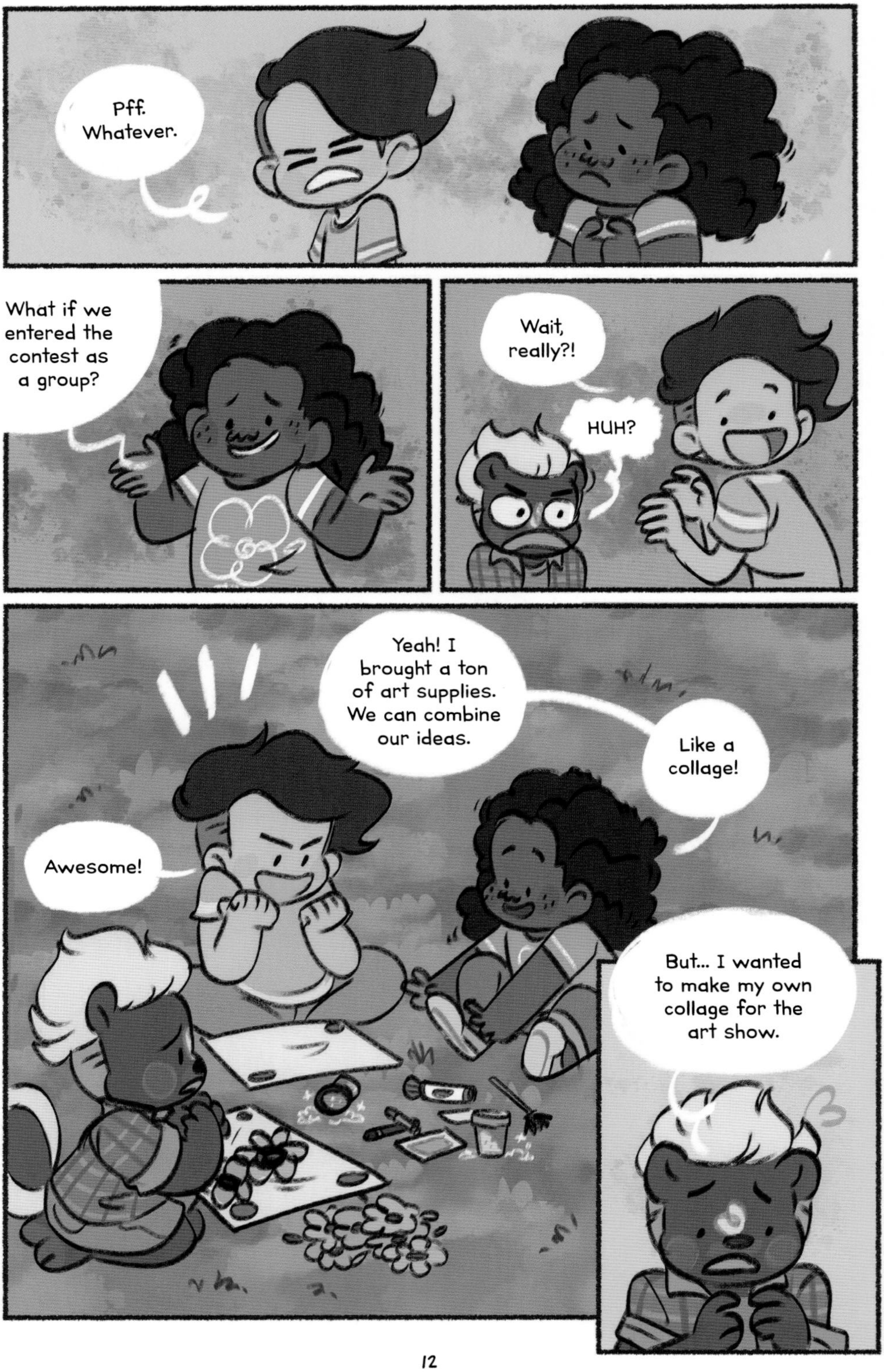
Pff.
Whatever.
What if we entered the contest as a group?
Wait, really?!
HUH?
Yeah! I brought a ton of art supplies. We can combine our ideas.
Like a collage!
Awesome!
But... I wanted to make my own collage for the art show.

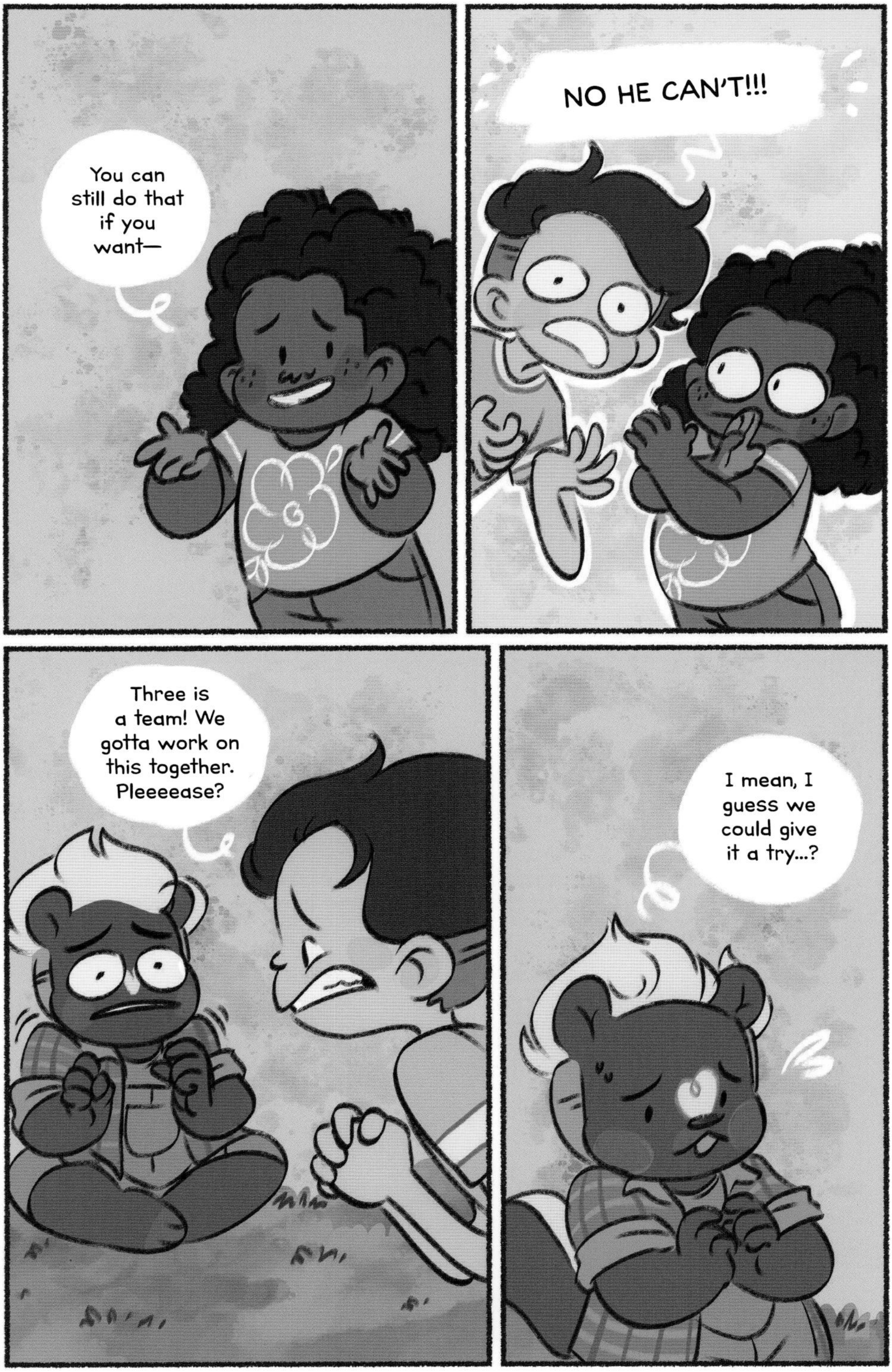

You can still do that if you want—
NO HE CAN'T!!!
Three is a team! We gotta work on this together. Pleeeease?
I mean, I guess we could give it a try...?

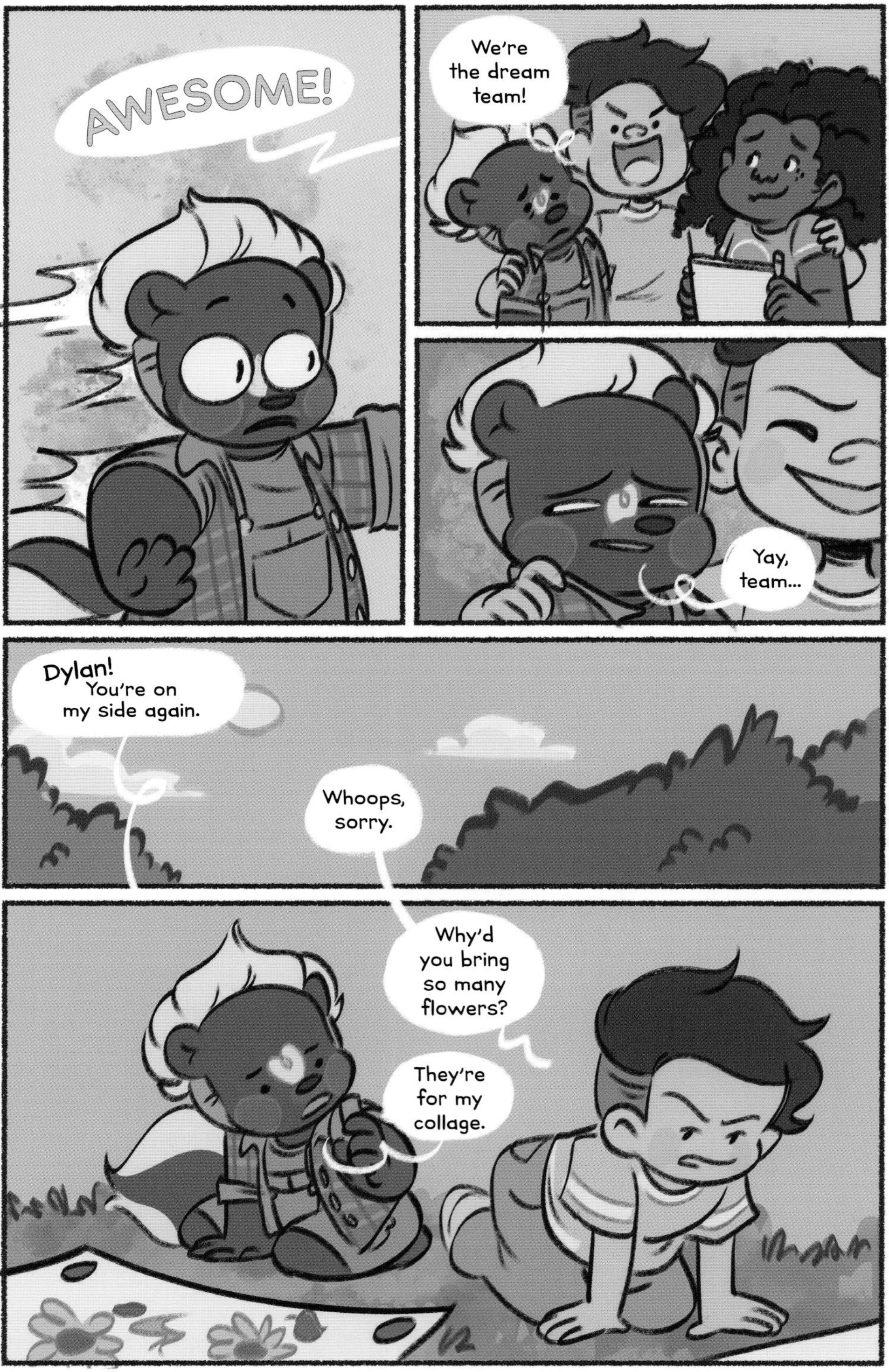
AWESOME!
We're the dream team!
Yay, team...
Dylan! You're on my side again.
Whoops, sorry.
Why'd you bring so many flowers?
They're for my collage.

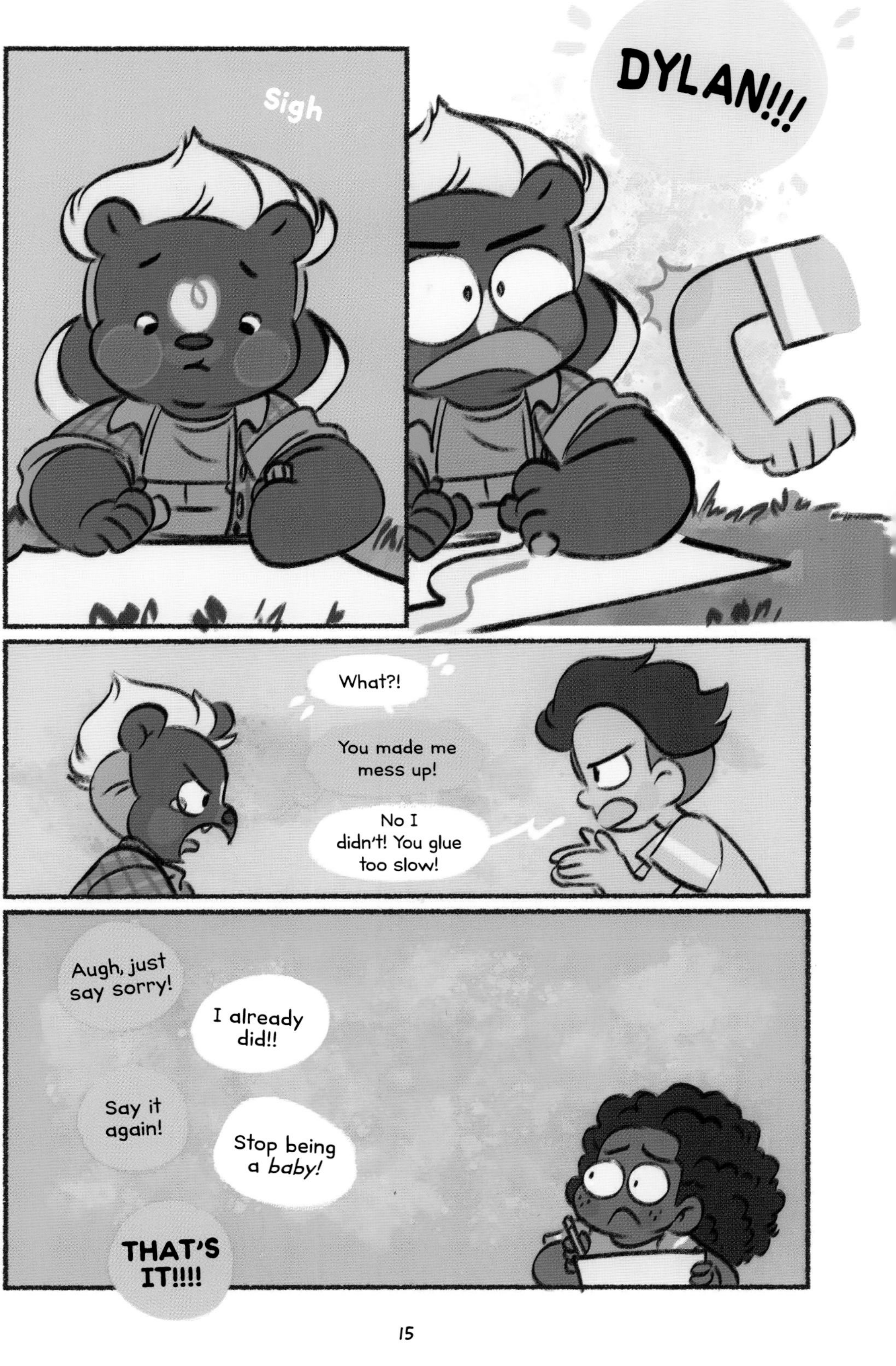
Sigh
DYLAN!!!
What?!
You made me mess up!
No I didn't! You glue too slow!
Augh, just say sorry!
I already did!!
Say it again!
Stop being a *baby!*
THAT'S IT!!!!

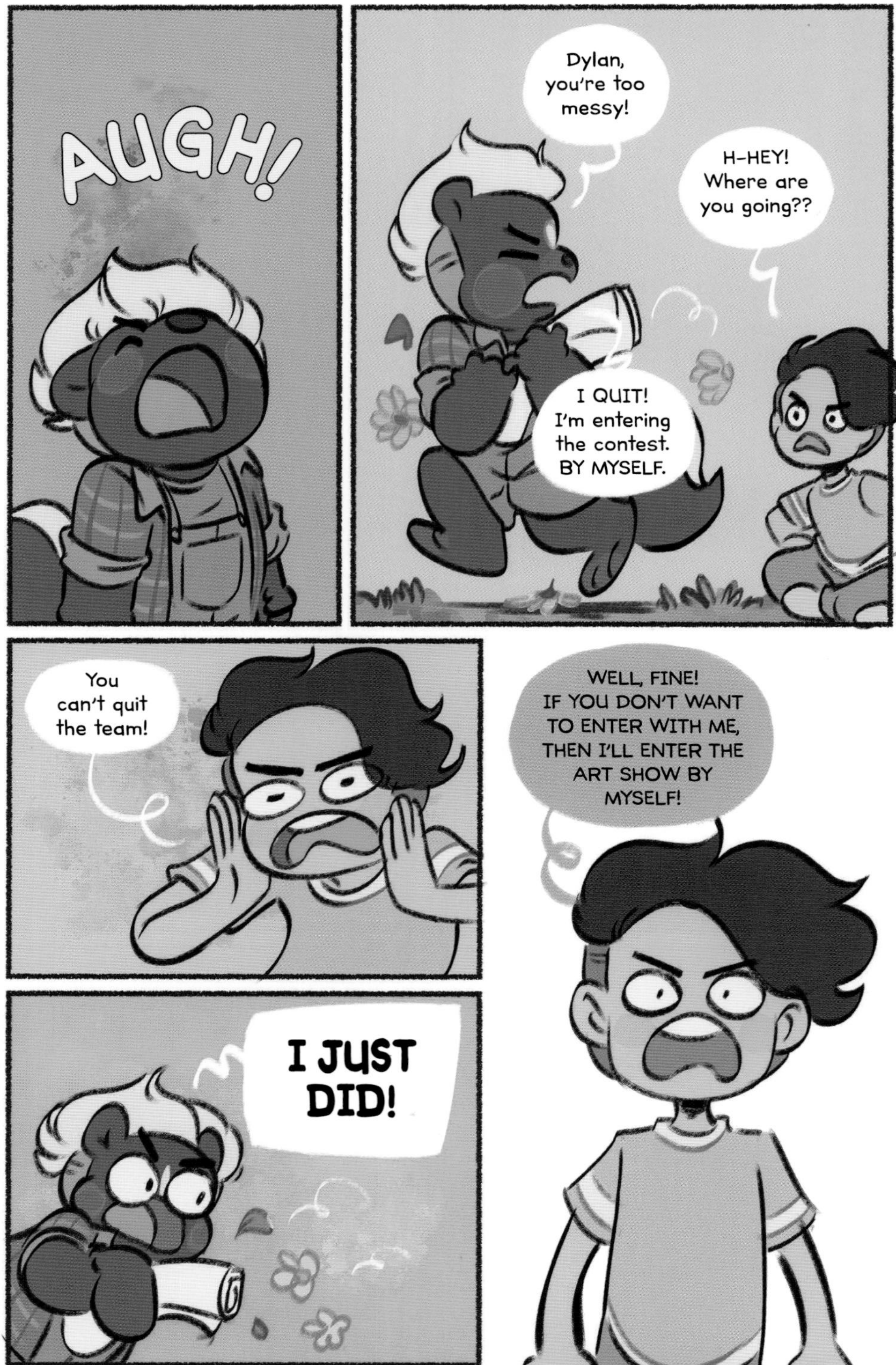
AUGH!
Dylan, you're too messy!
H-HEY! Where are you going??
I QUIT! I'm entering the contest. BY MYSELF.
You can't quit the team!
I JUST DID!
WELL, FINE! IF YOU DON'T WANT TO ENTER WITH ME, THEN I'LL ENTER THE ART SHOW BY MYSELF!

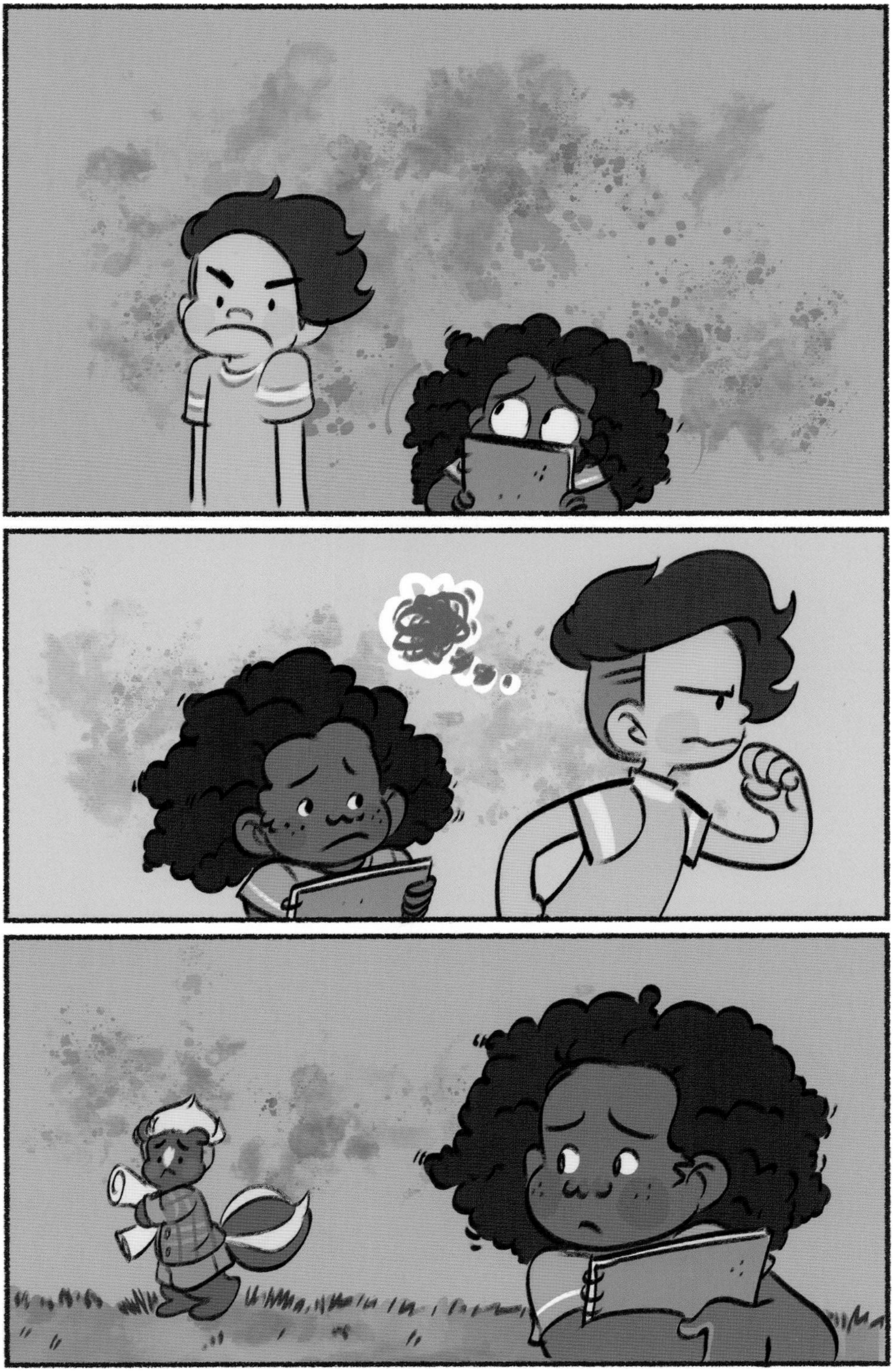

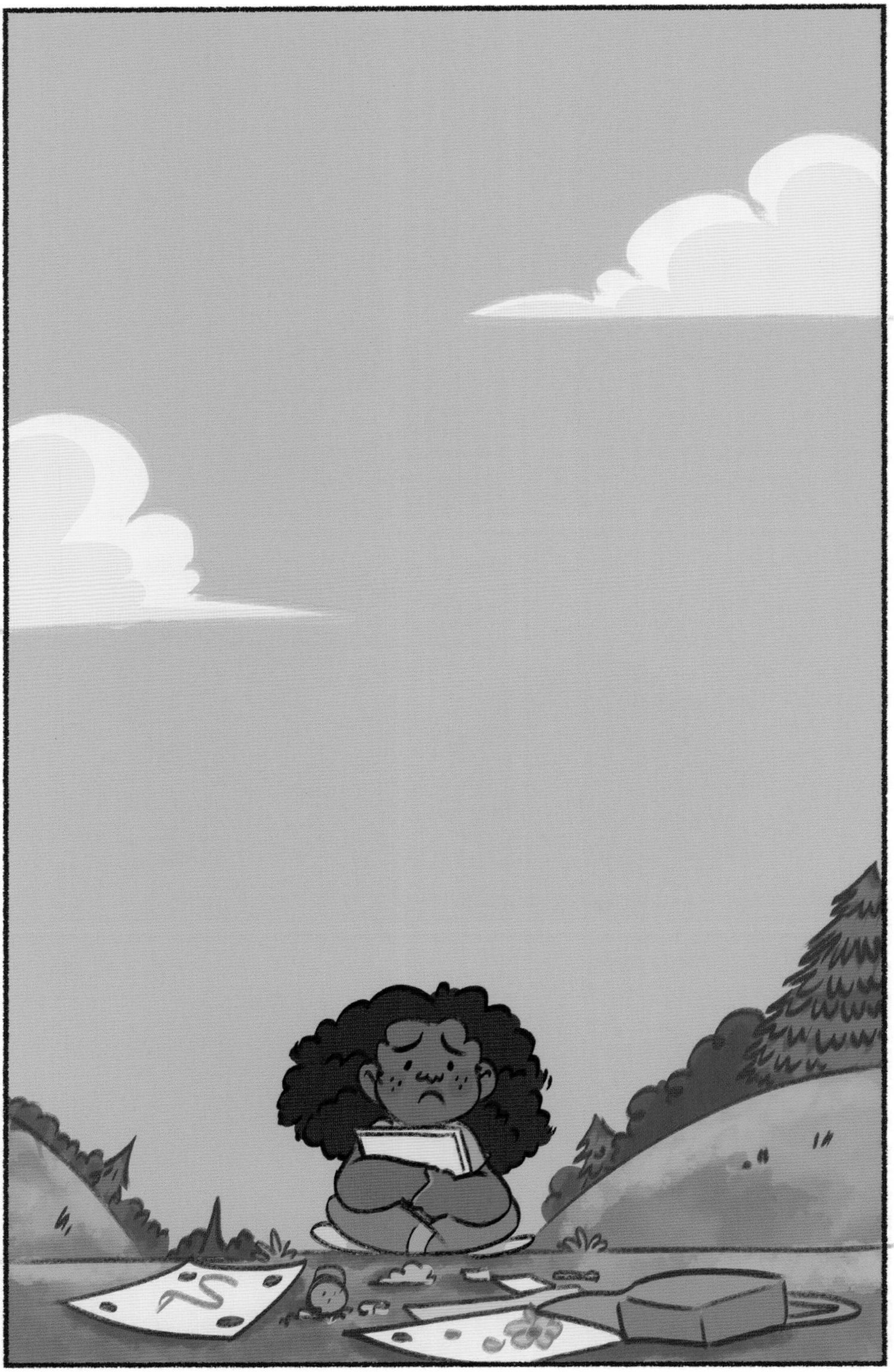

CHAPTER 2

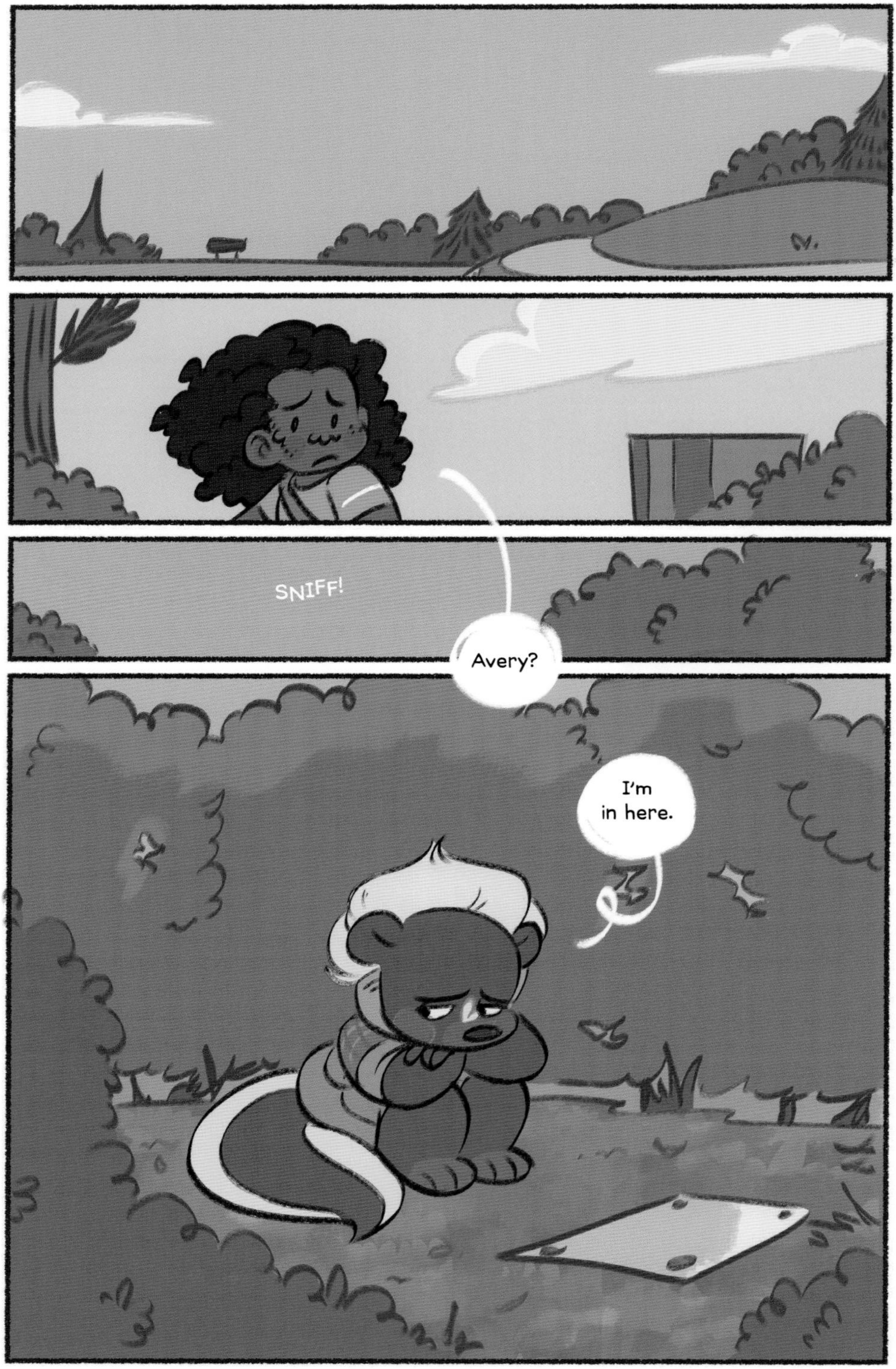
SNIFF!
Avery?
I'm
in here.

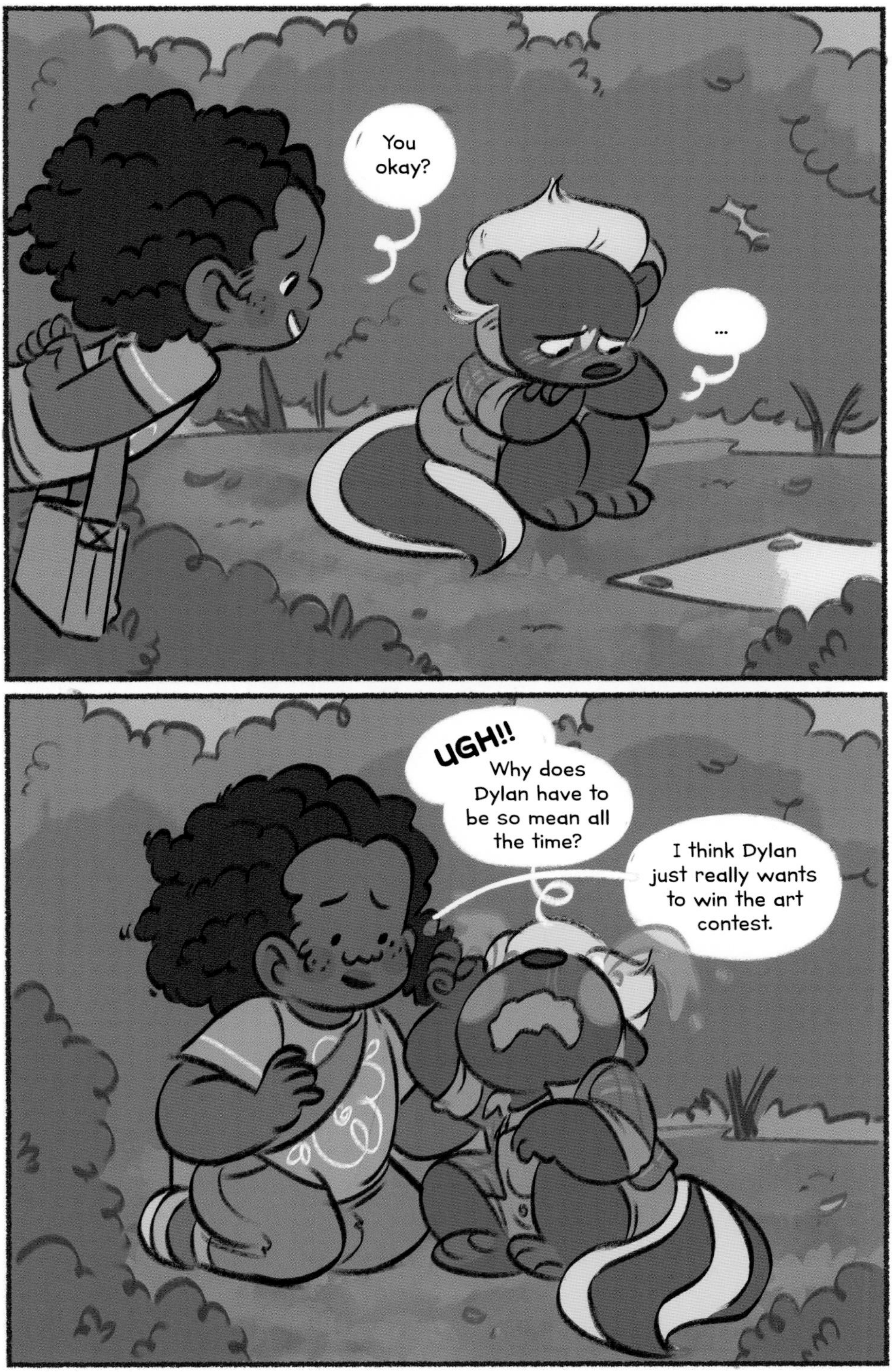
You okay?
...
UGH!! Why does Dylan have to be so mean all the time?
I think Dylan just really wants to win the art contest.

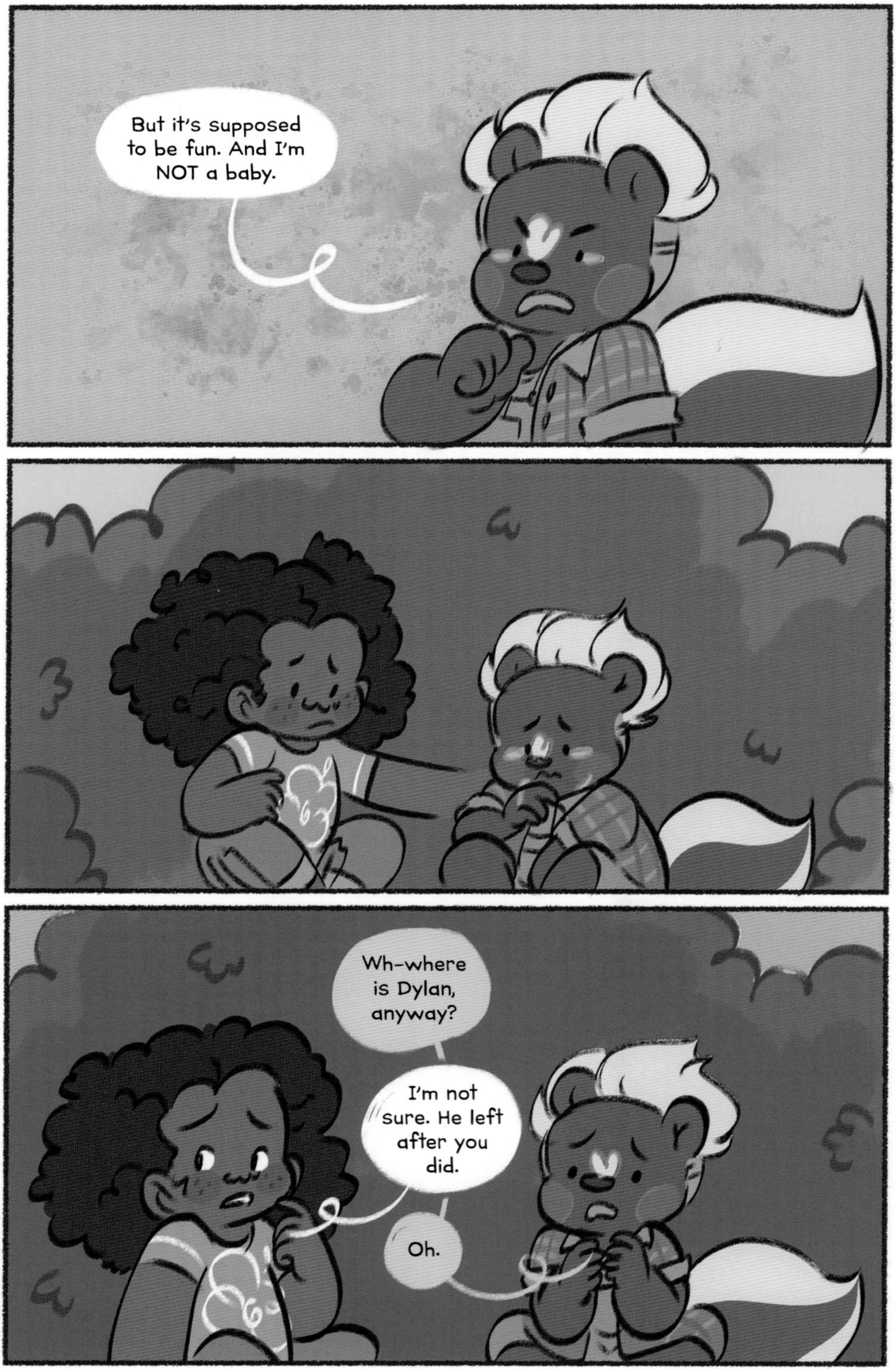
But it's supposed to be fun. And I'm NOT a baby.
Wh-where is Dylan, anyway?
I'm not sure. He left after you did.
Oh.

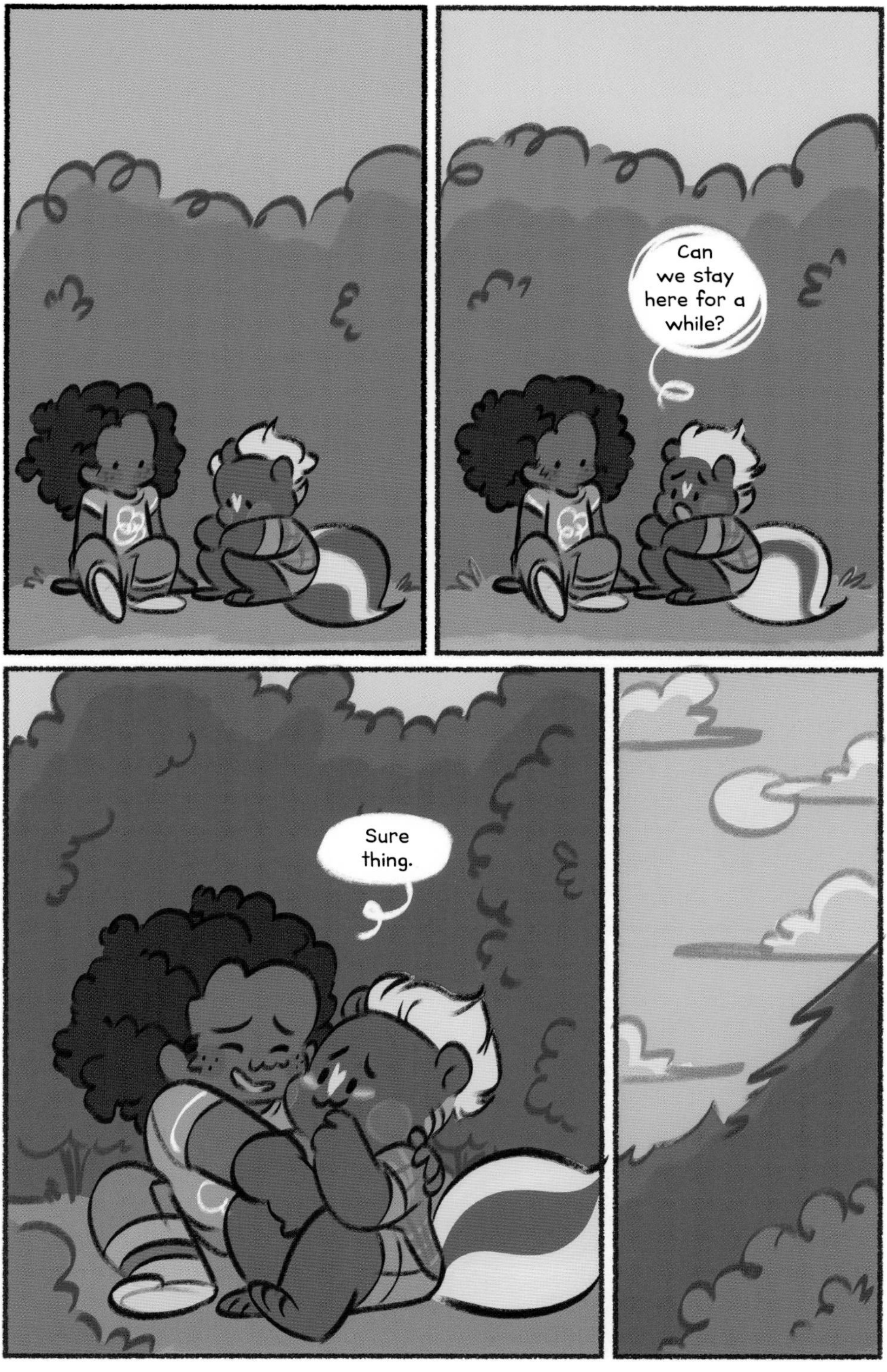
Can we stay here for a while?
Sure thing.

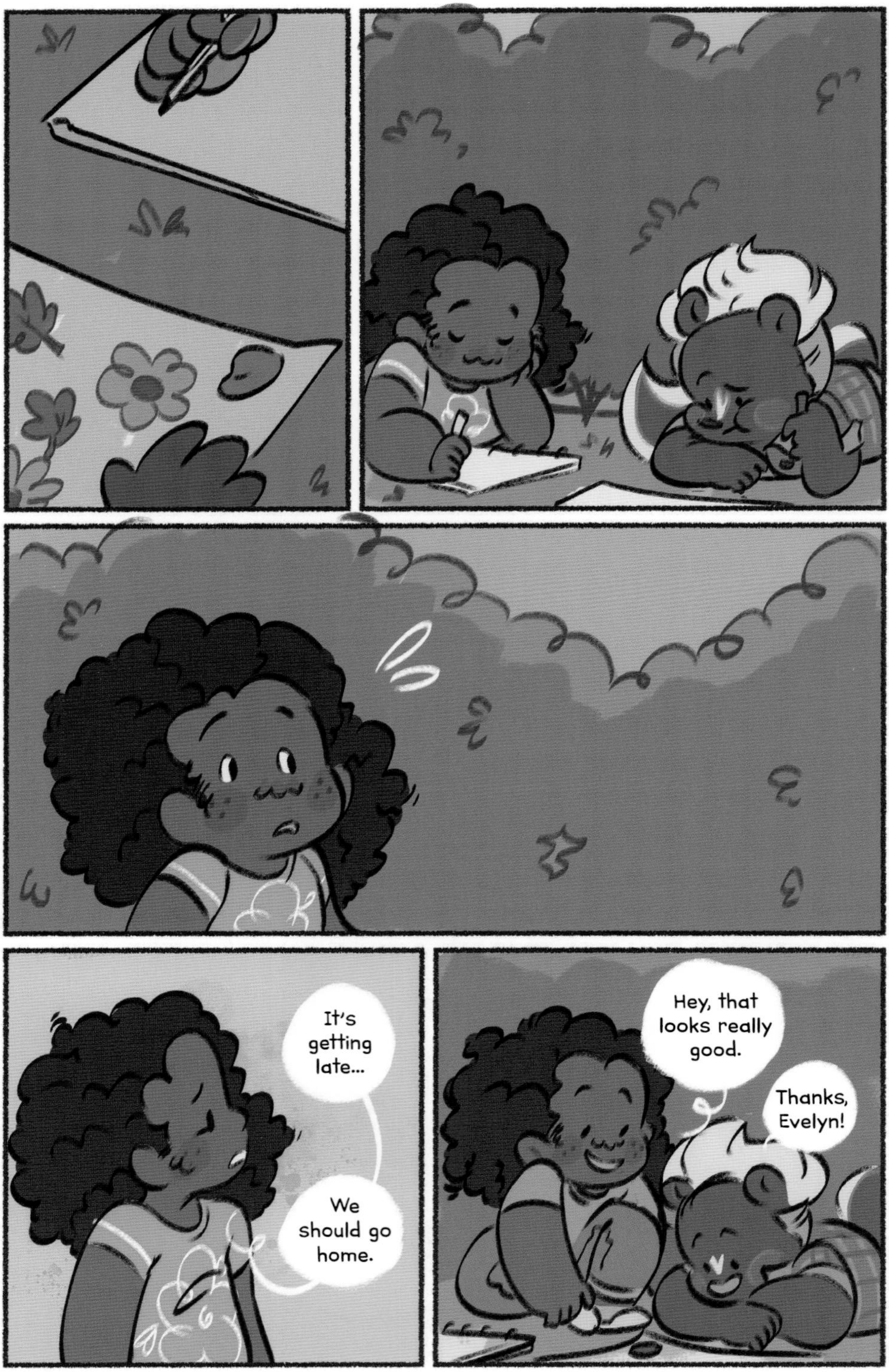
It's getting late...
We should go home.
Hey, that looks really good.
Thanks, Evelyn!

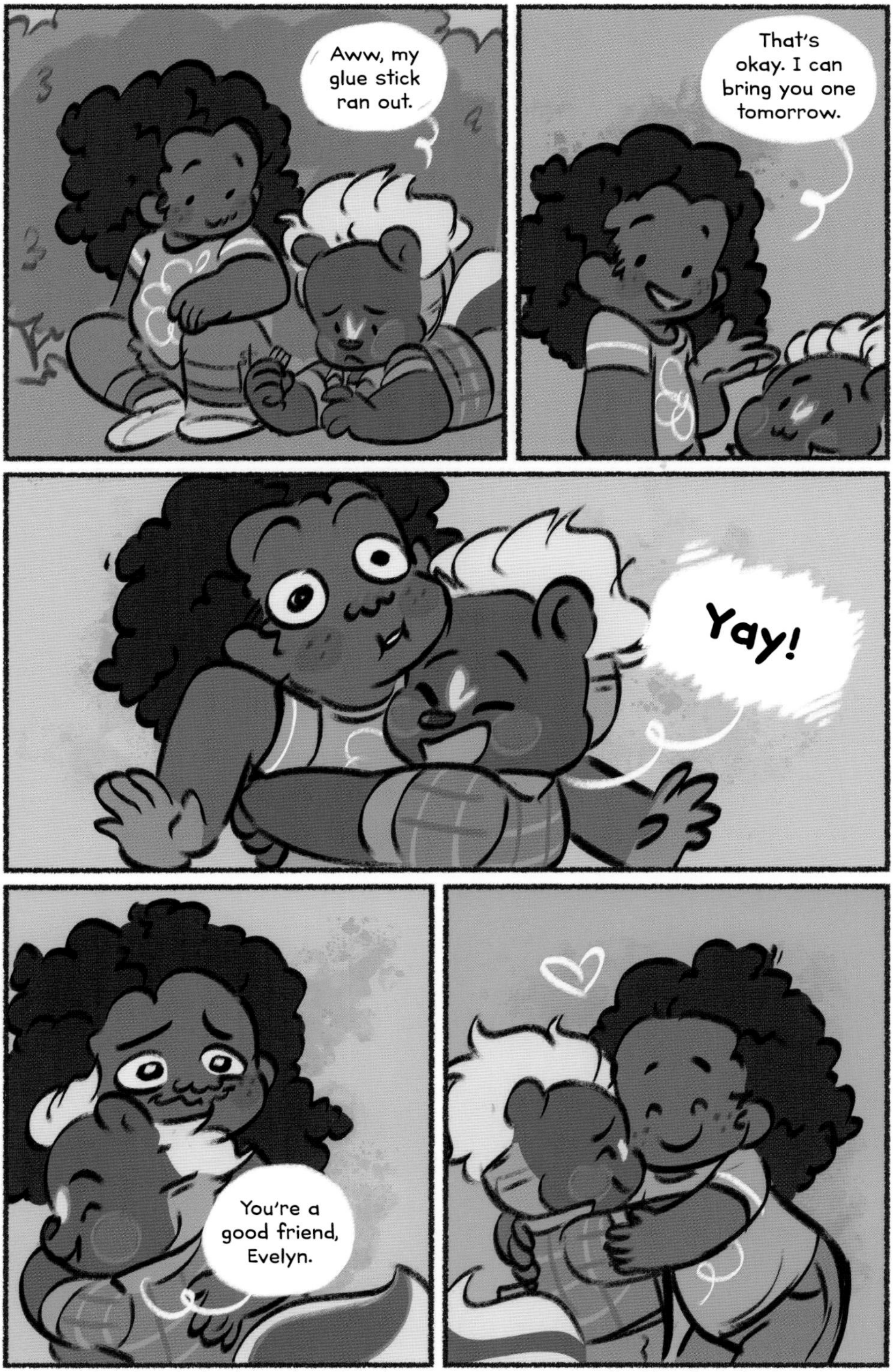
Aww, my glue stick ran out.
That's okay. I can bring you one tomorrow.
Yay!
You're a good friend, Evelyn.

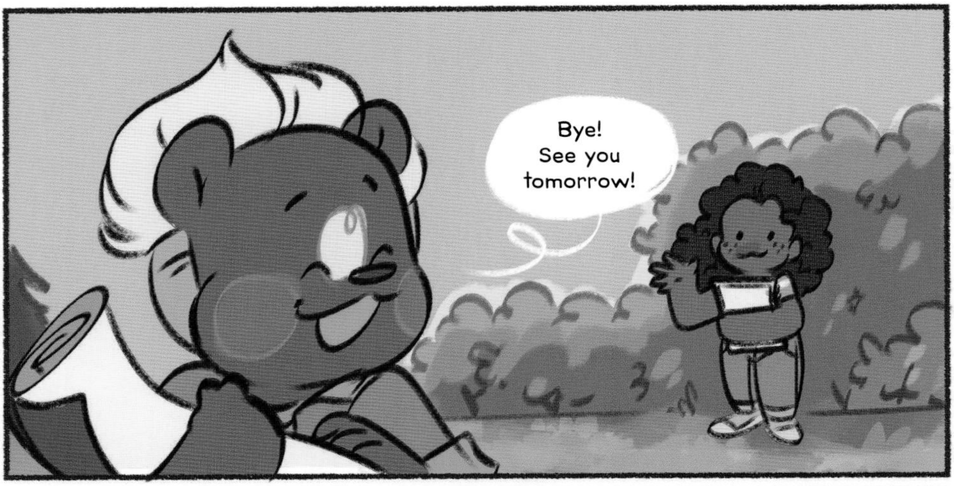
Bye!
See you
tomorrow!

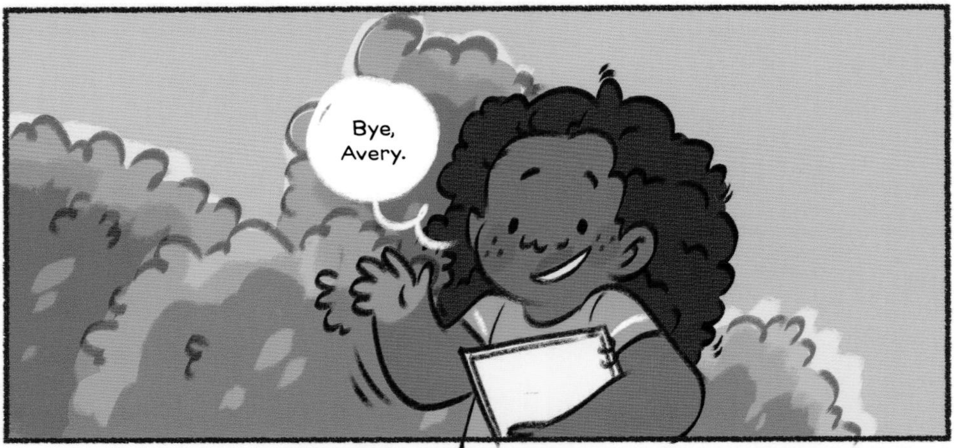
Bye,
Avery.

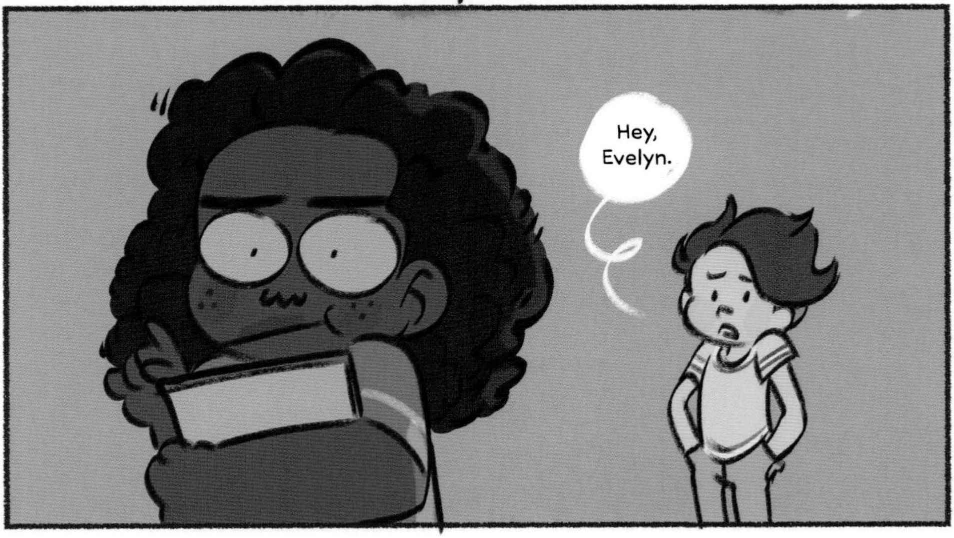
Hey,
Evelyn.

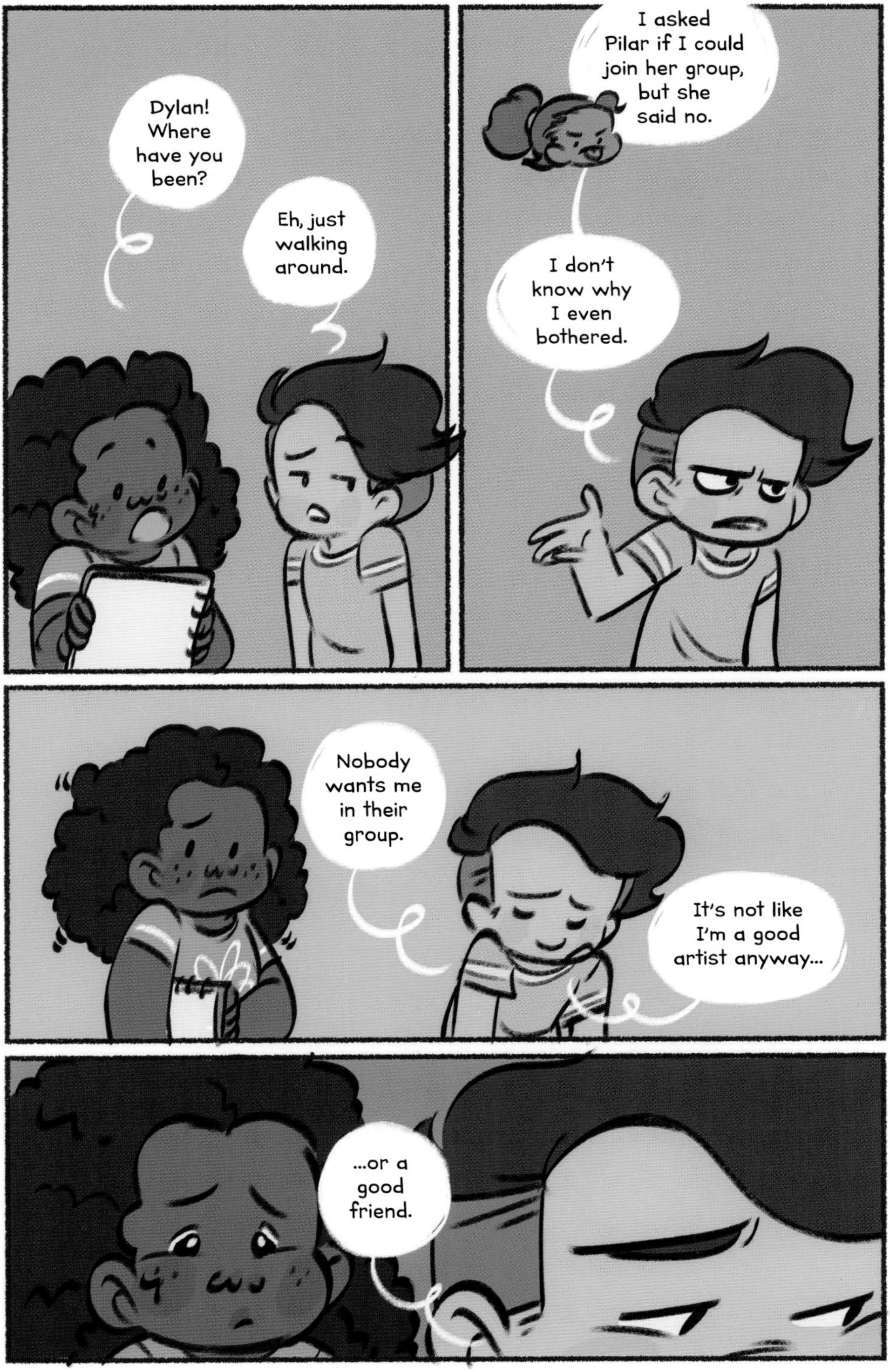
Dylan! Where have you been?
Eh, just walking around.
I asked Pilar if I could join her group, but she said no.
I don't know why I even bothered.
Nobody wants me in their group.
It's not like I'm a good artist anyway...
...or a good friend.

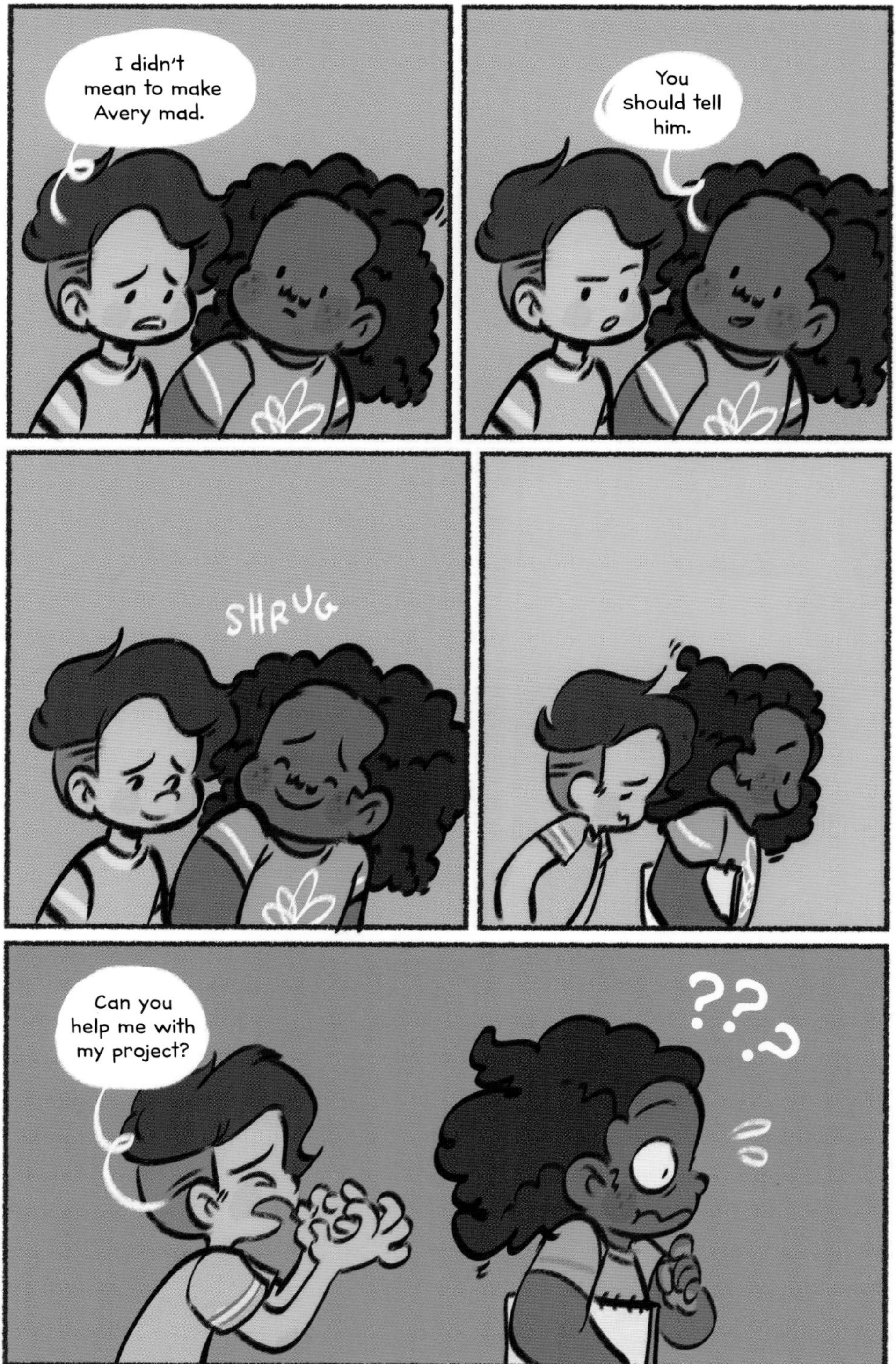
I didn't mean to make Avery mad.
You should tell him.
SHRUG
Can you help me with my project?
???

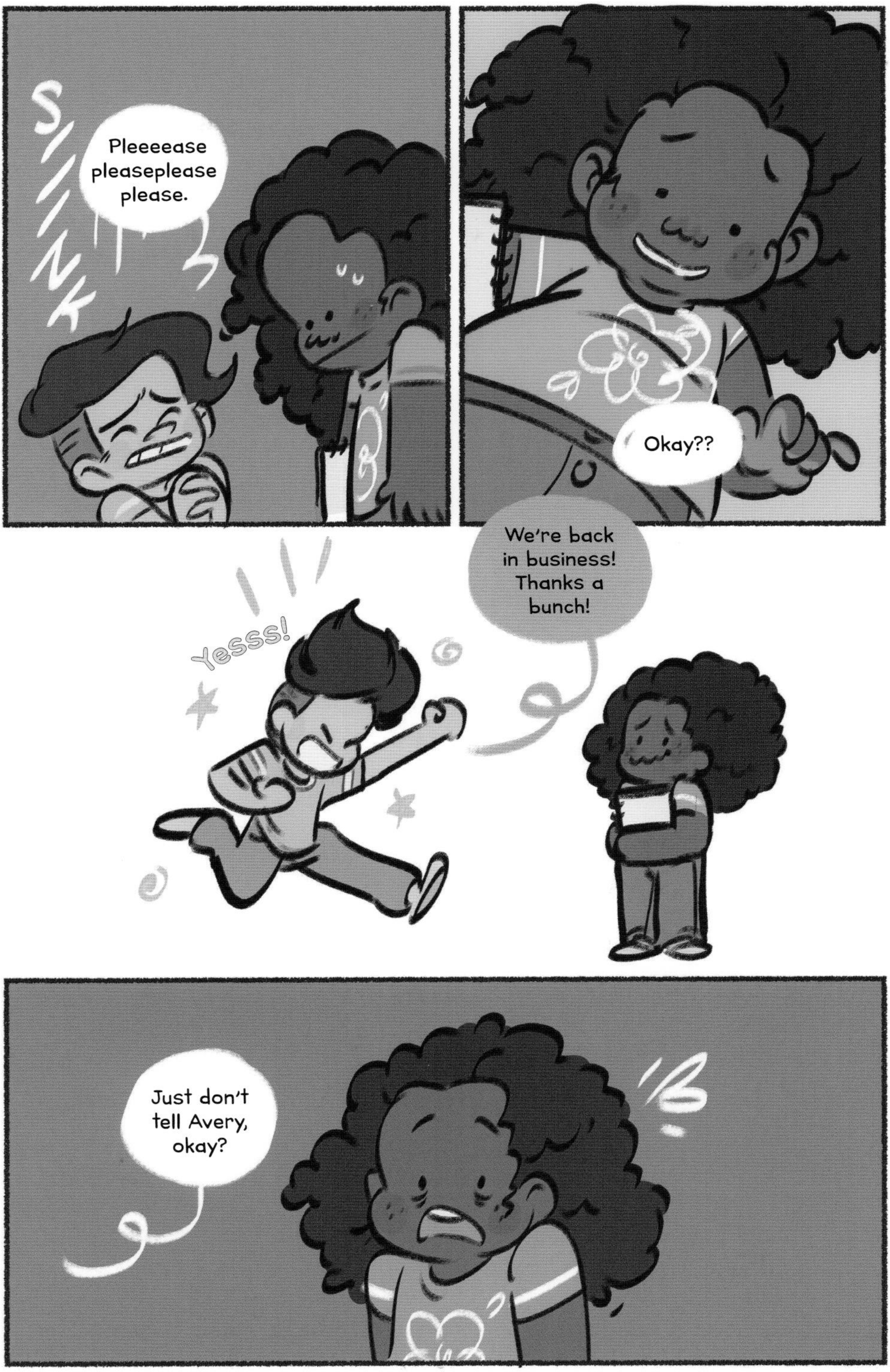
SINK
Pleeeease pleaseplease please.
Okay??
Yesss!
We're back in business! Thanks a bunch!
Just don't tell Avery, okay?

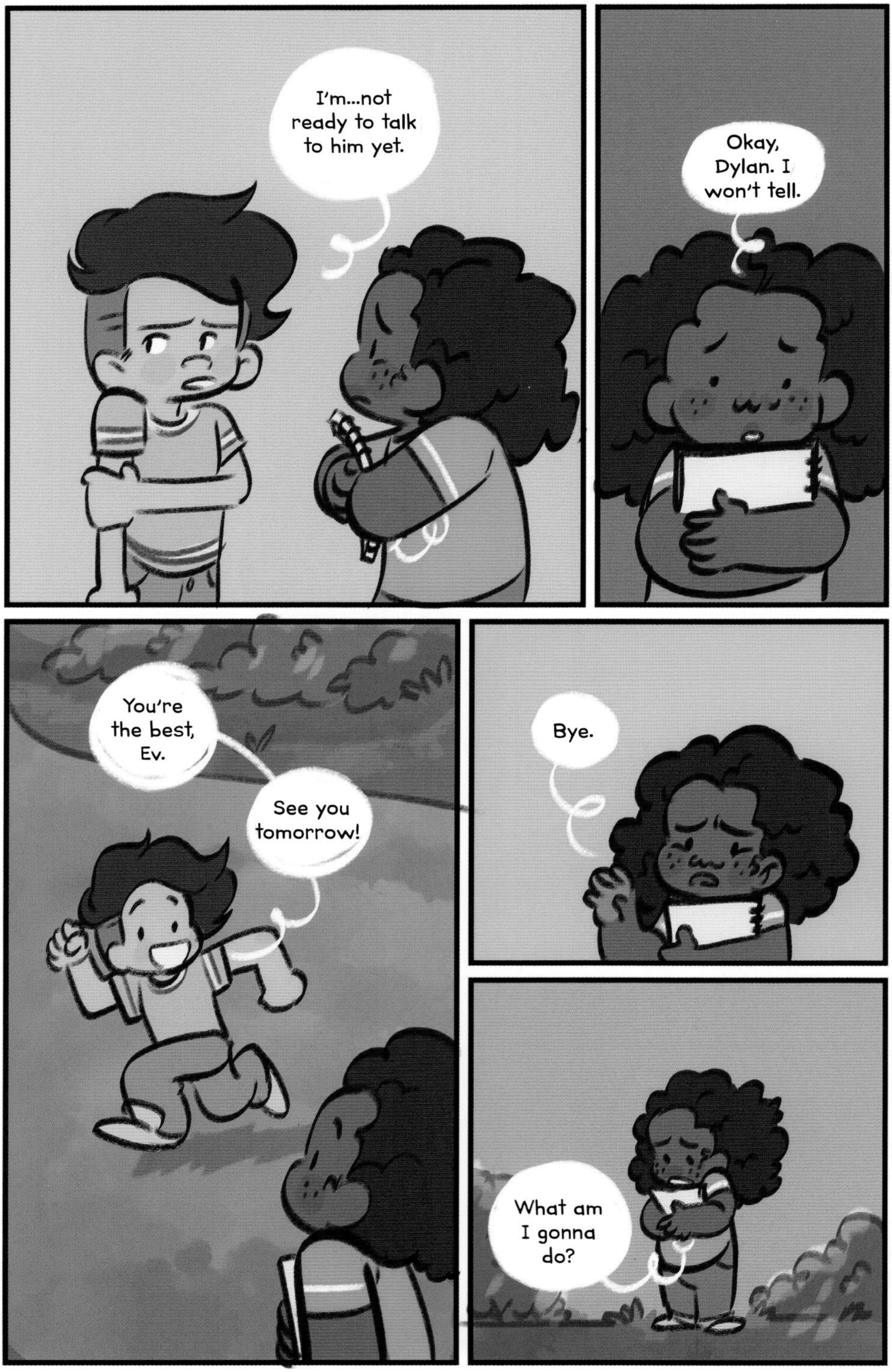
I'm...not ready to talk to him yet.
Okay, Dylan. I won't tell.
You're the best, Ev.
See you tomorrow!
Bye.
What am I gonna do?

CHAPTER 3

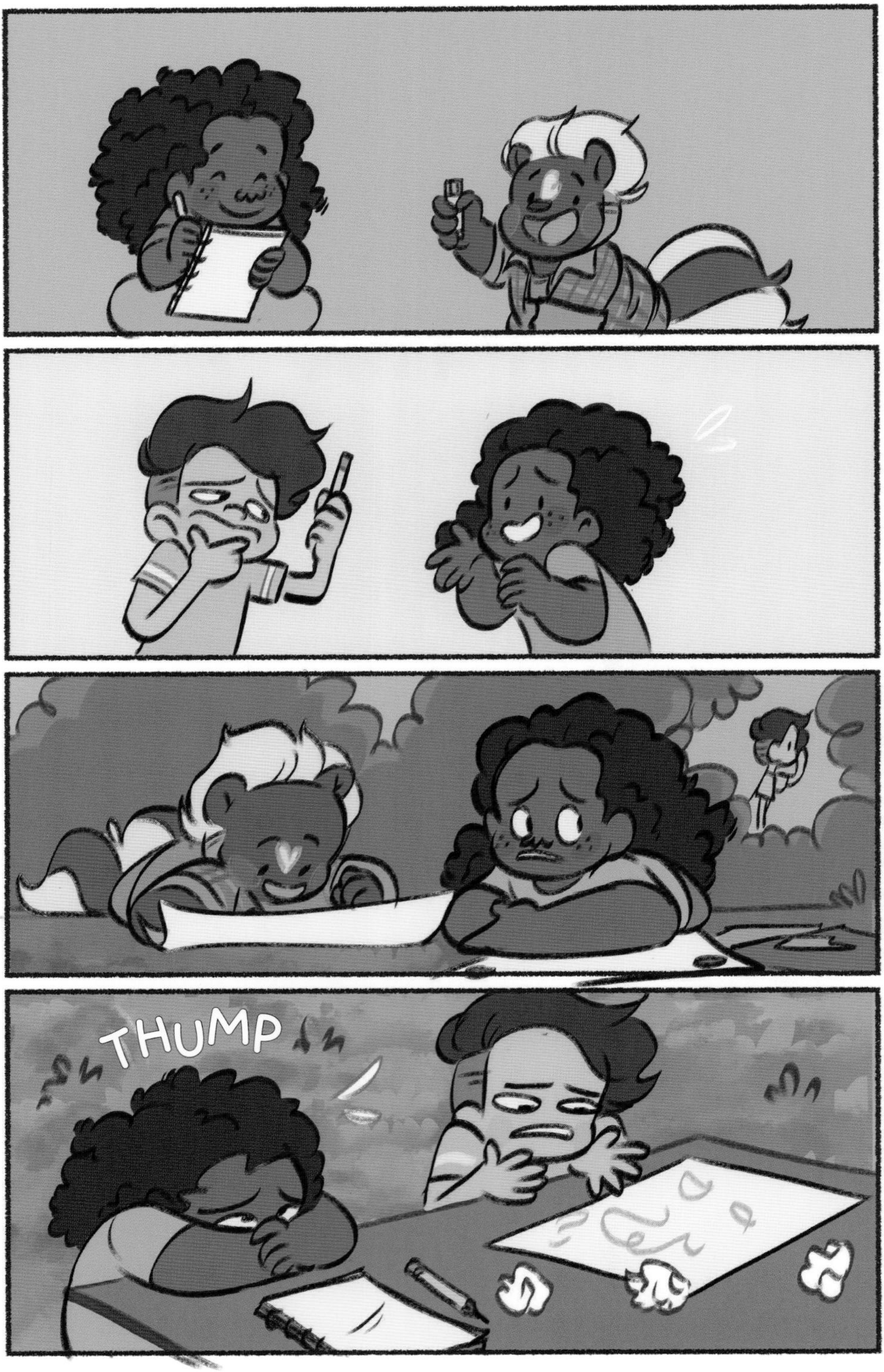
THUMP

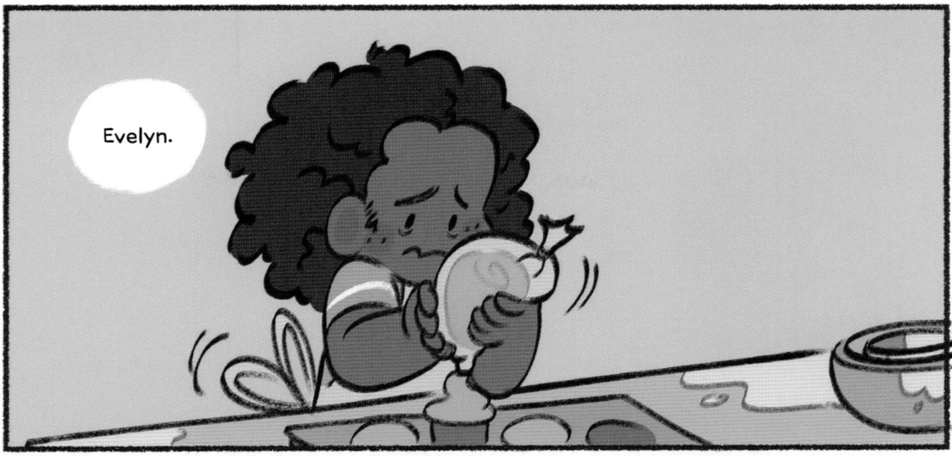
Evelyn.

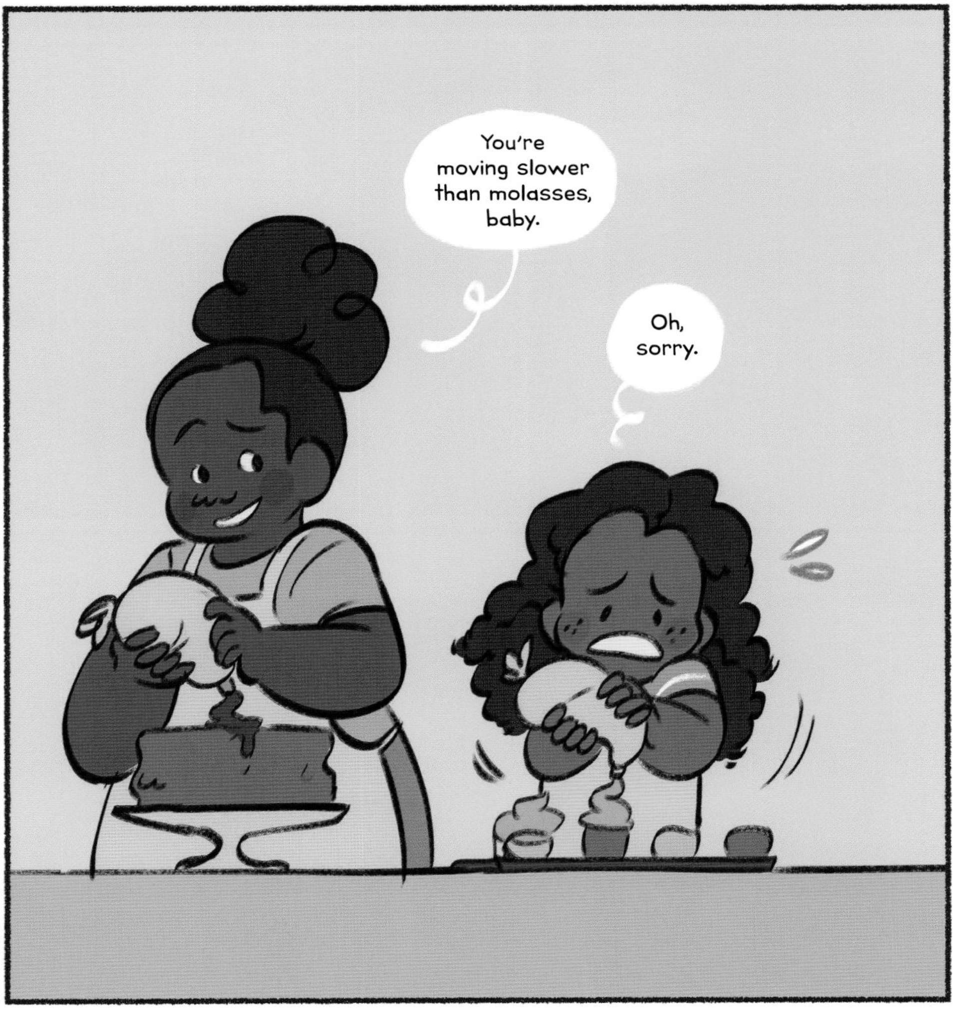
You're moving slower than molasses, baby.
Oh, sorry.

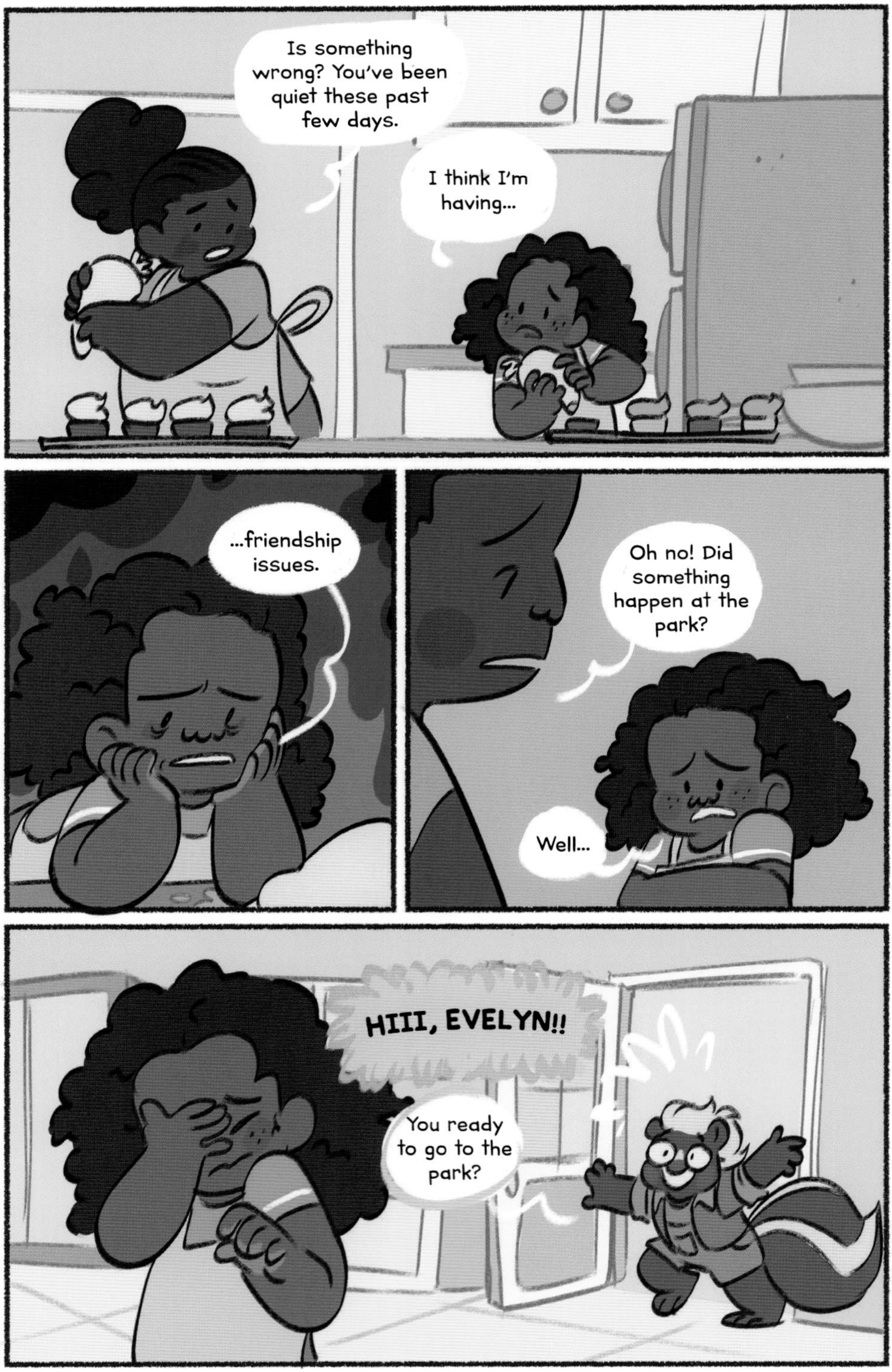
Is something wrong? You've been quiet these past few days.
I think I'm having...
...friendship issues.
Oh no! Did something happen at the park?
Well...
HIII, EVELYN!!
You ready to go to the park?

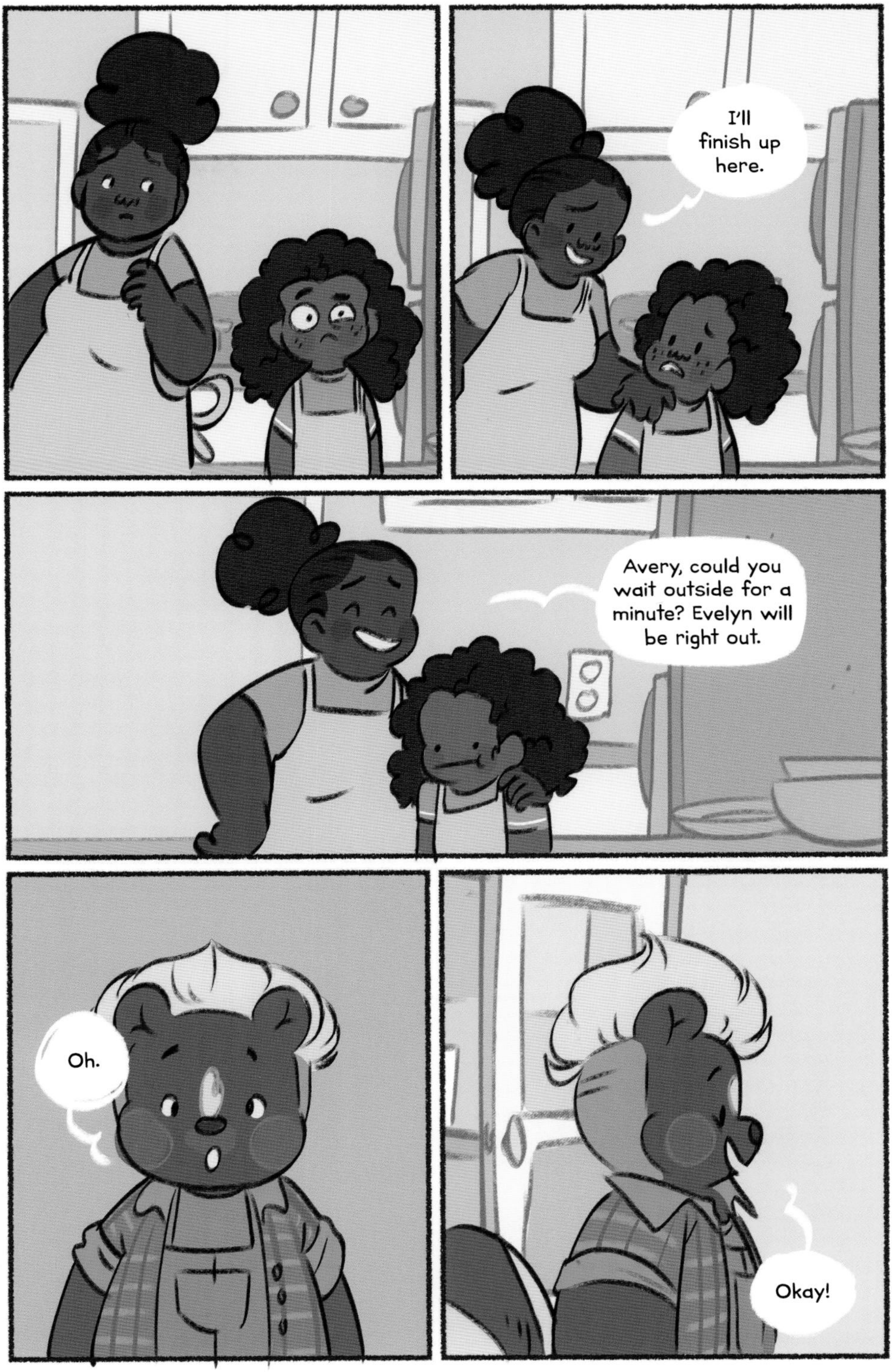
I'll finish up here.
Avery, could you wait outside for a minute? Evelyn will be right out.
Oh.
Okay!

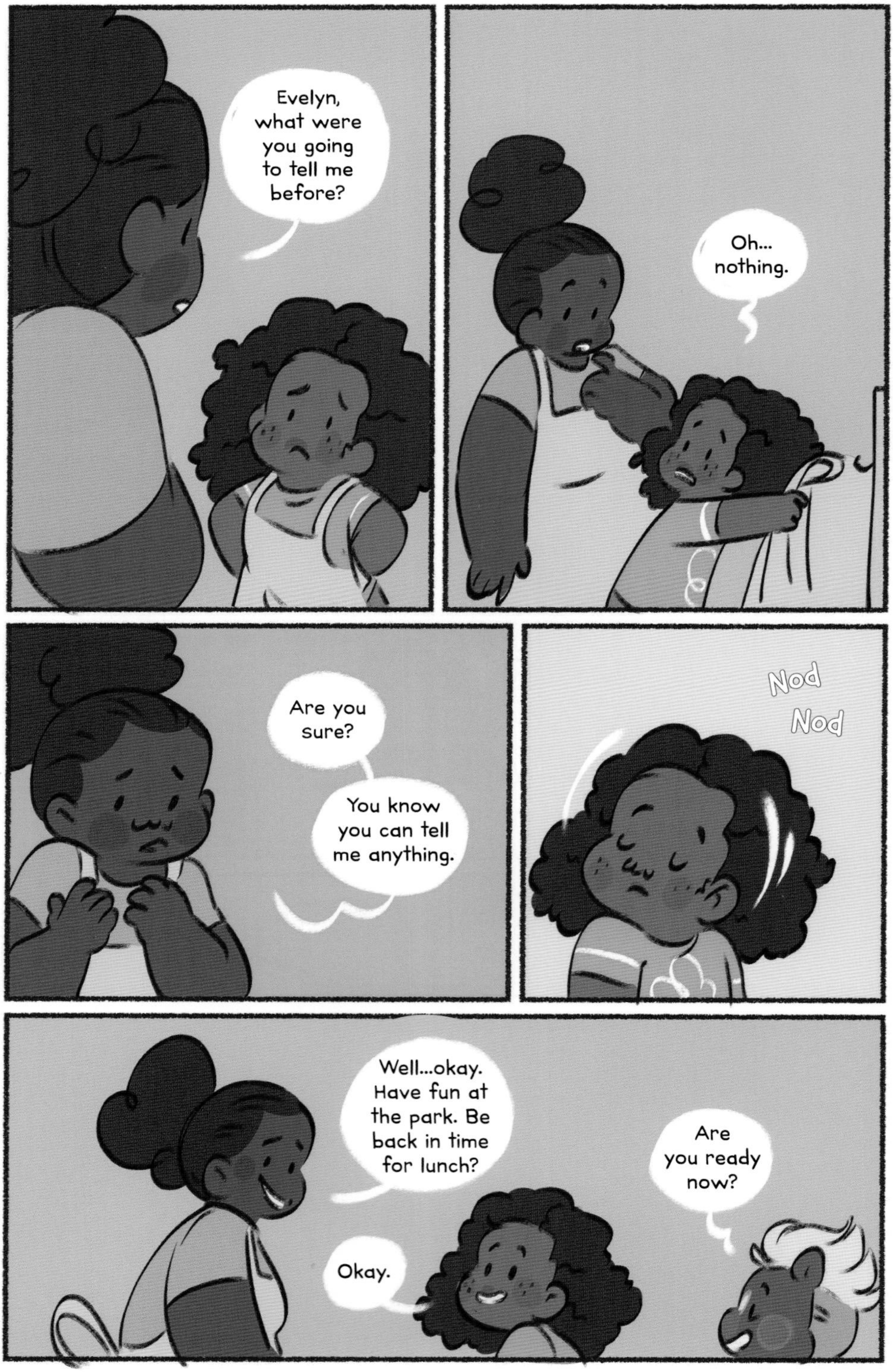
Evelyn, what were you going to tell me before?
Oh... nothing.
Are you sure?
You know you can tell me anything.
Nod
Nod
Well...okay. Have fun at the park. Be back in time for lunch?
Okay.
Are you ready now?

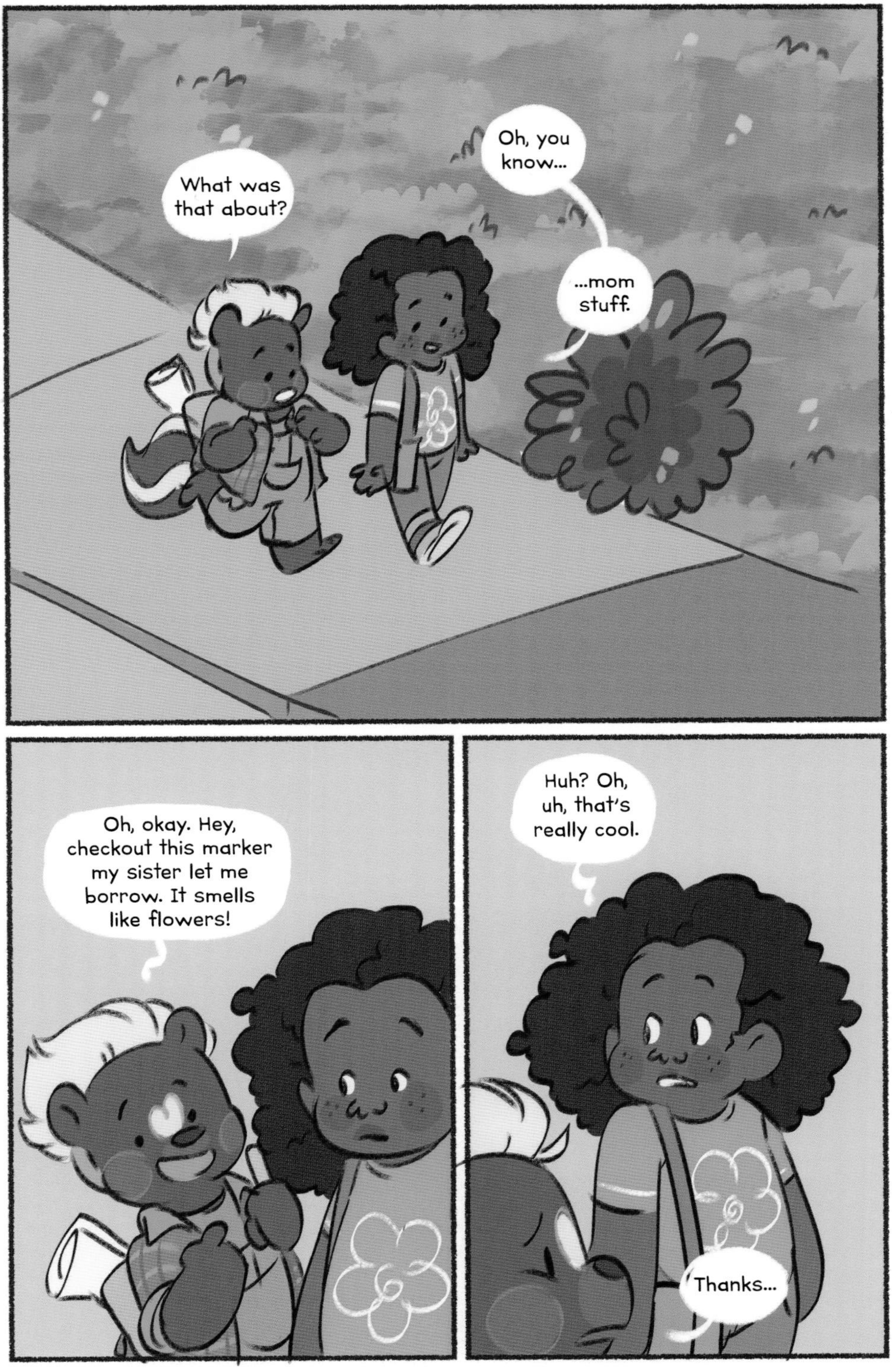
What was that about?
Oh, you know...
...mom stuff.
Oh, okay. Hey, checkout this marker my sister let me borrow. It smells like flowers!
Huh? Oh, uh, that's really cool.
Thanks...

Evelyn!

What are you doing?!

Huh??

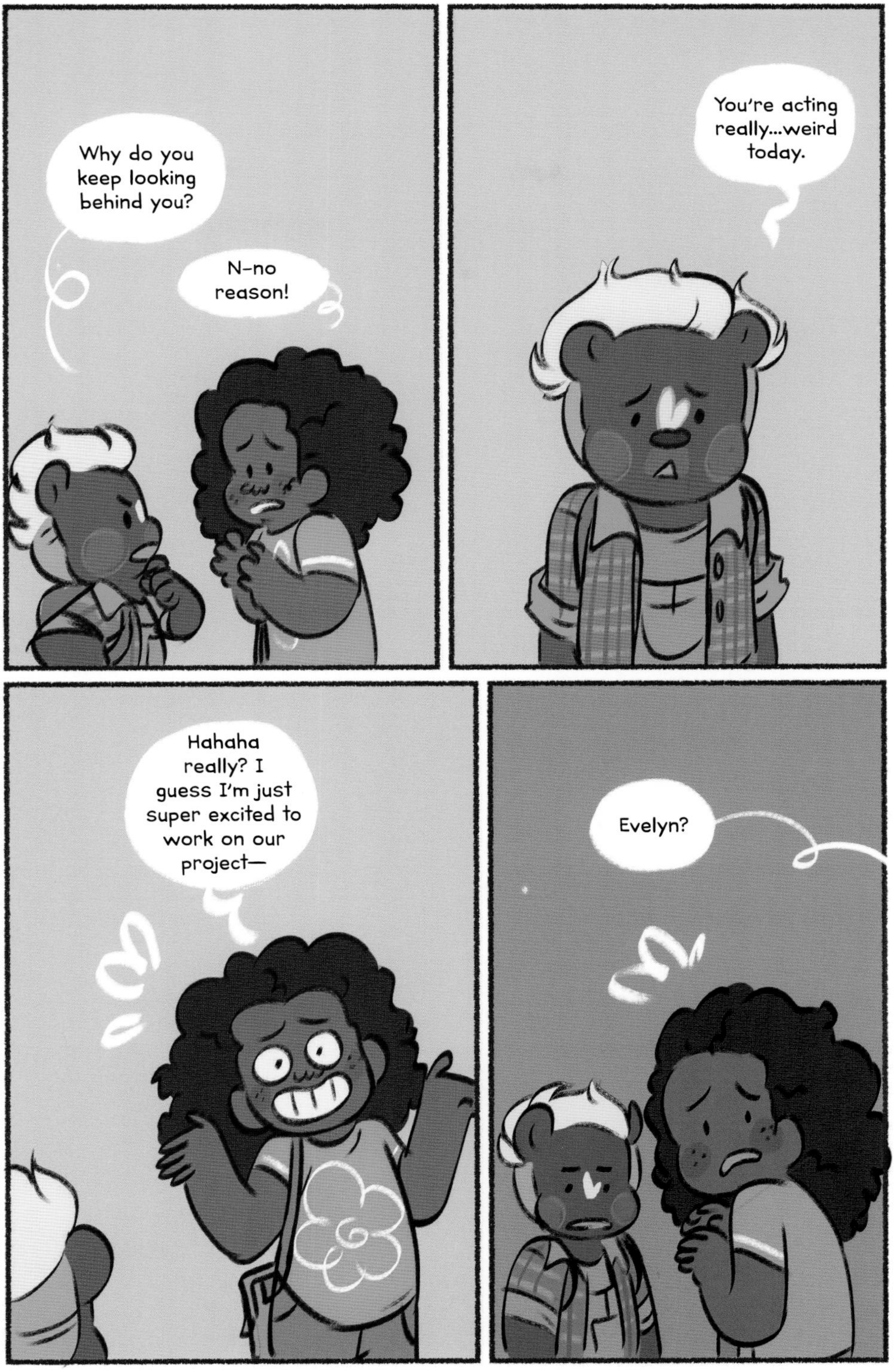
Why do you keep looking behind you?
N-no reason!
You're acting really...weird today.
Hahaha really? I guess I'm just super excited to work on our project—
Evelyn?

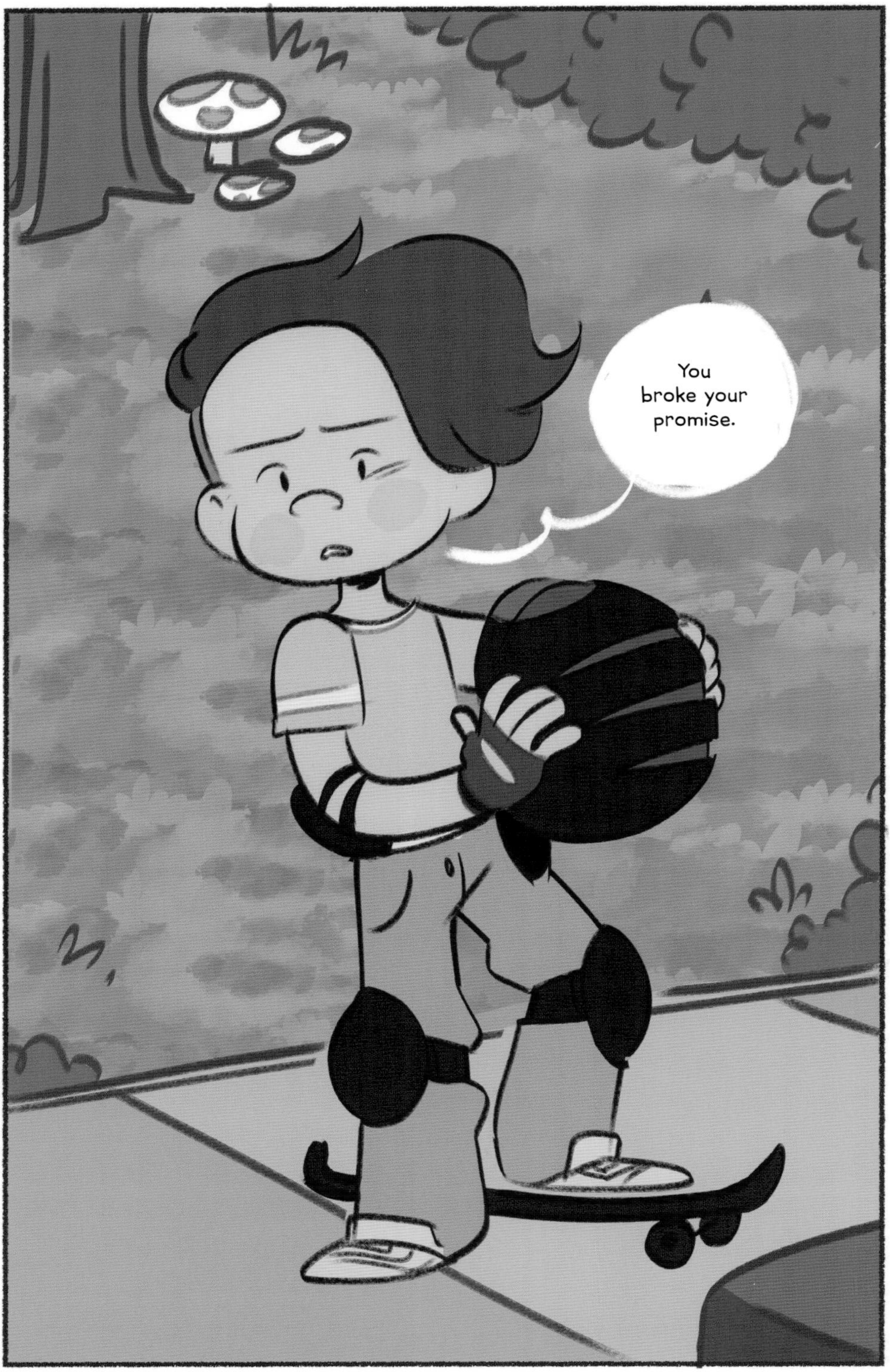
You broke your promise.

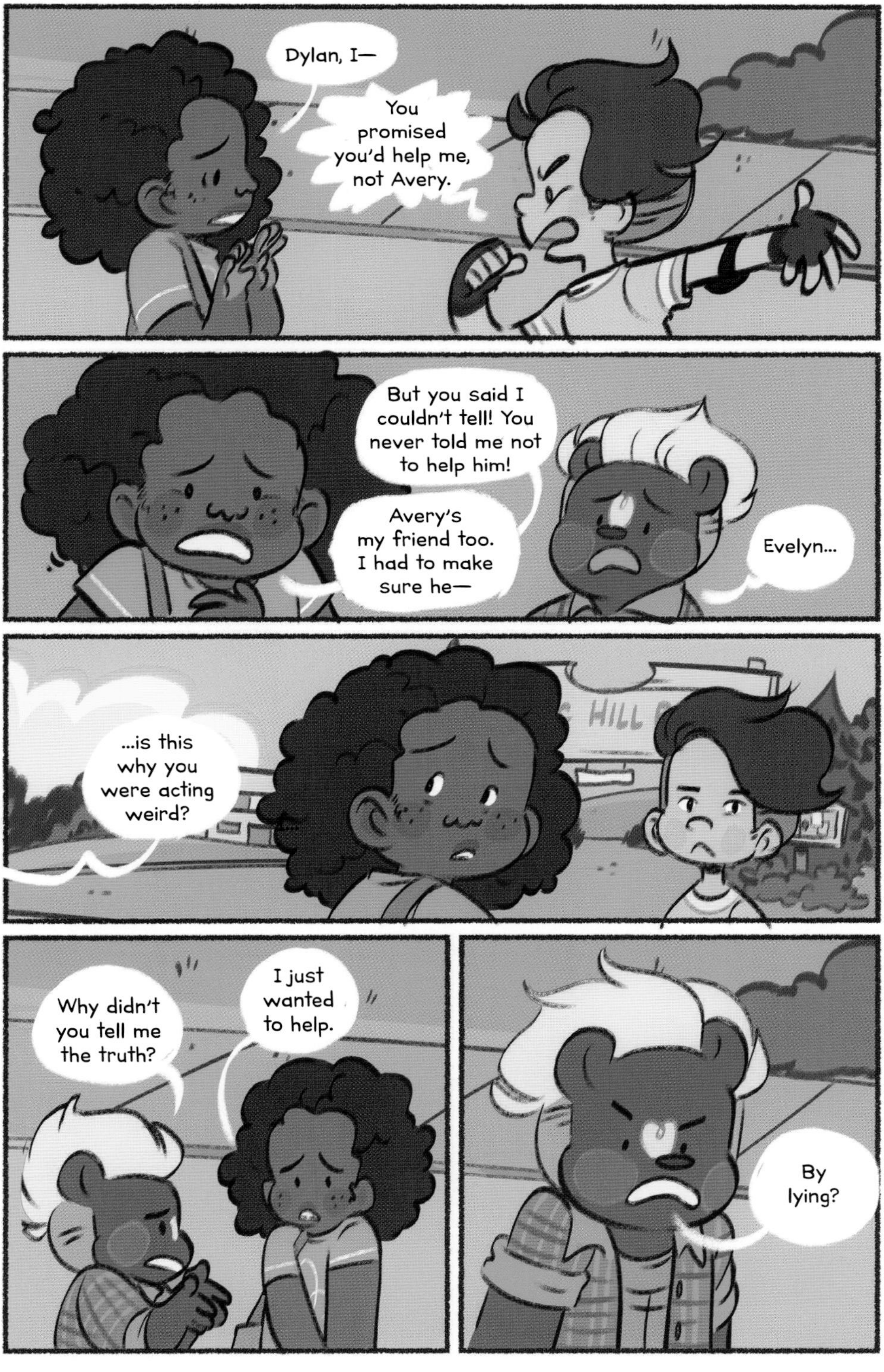
Dylan, I—
You promised you'd help me, not Avery.
But you said I couldn't tell! You never told me not to help him!
Avery's my friend too. I had to make sure he—
Evelyn...
...is this why you were acting weird?
HILL
Why didn't you tell me the truth?
I just wanted to help.
By lying?

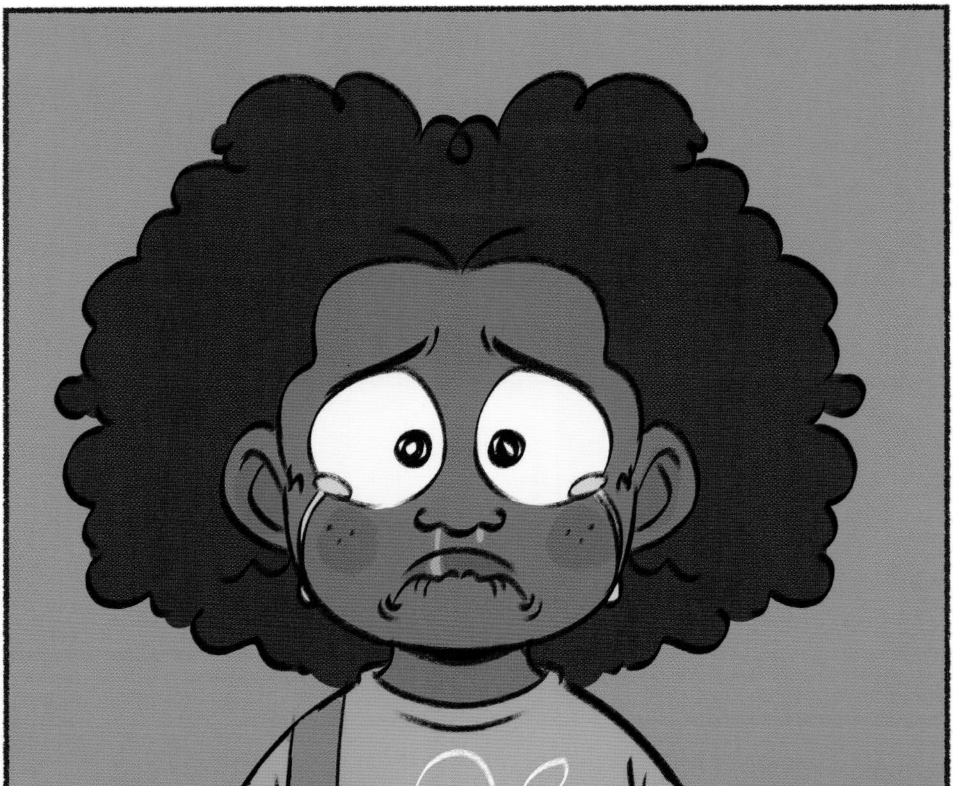

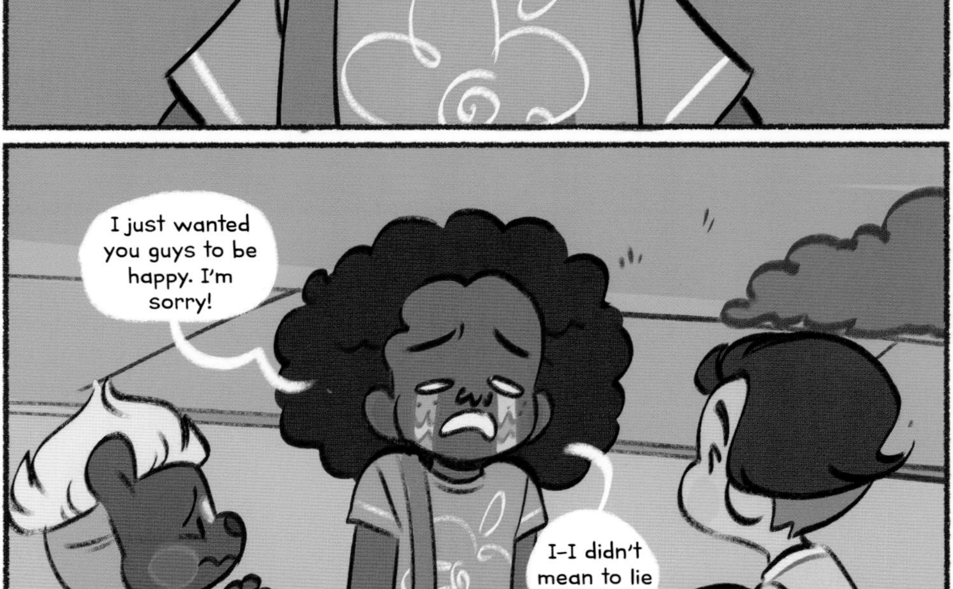
I just wanted you guys to be happy. I'm sorry!
I-I didn't mean to lie to you.

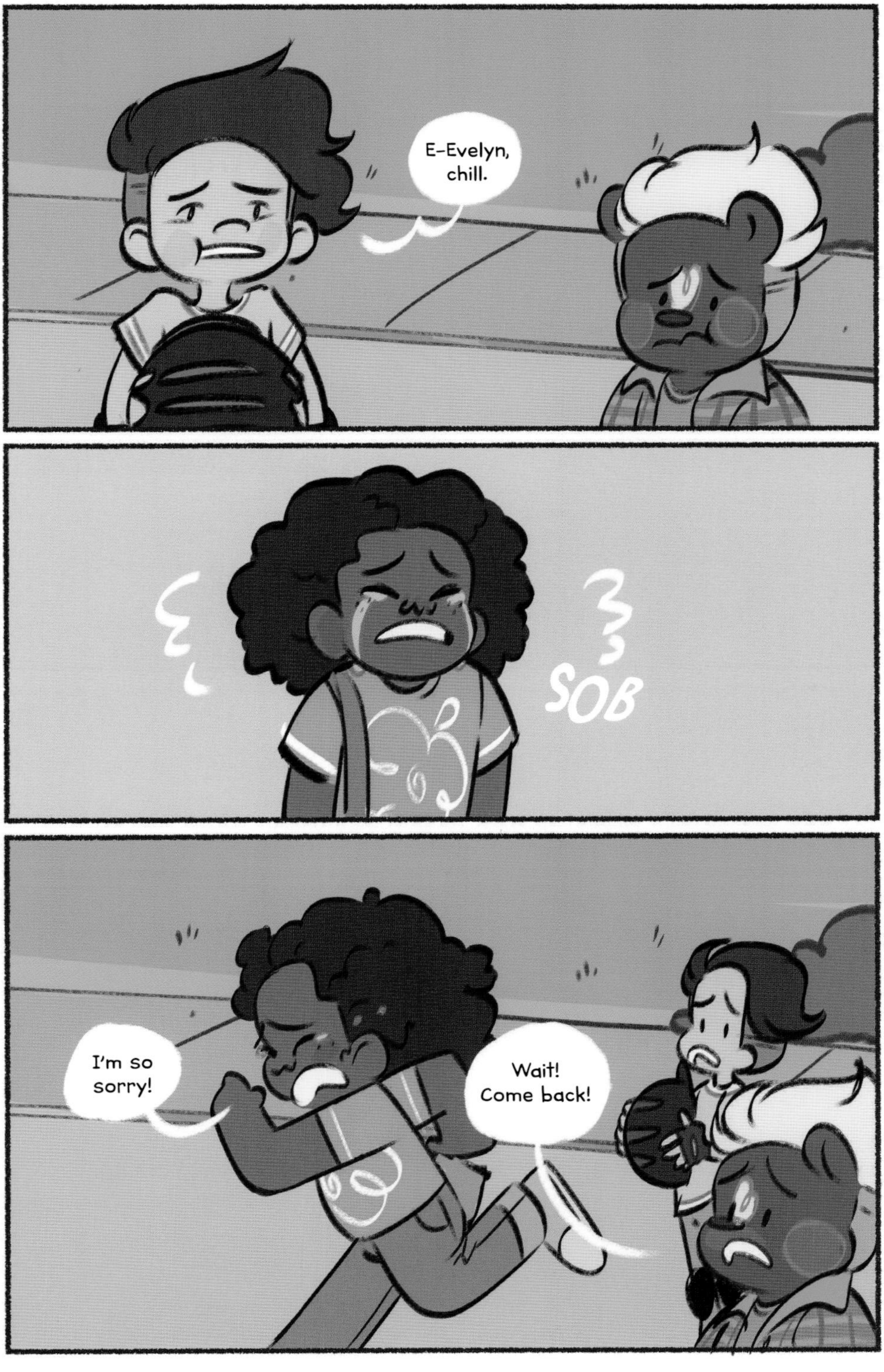
E-Evelyn, chill.
SOB
I'm so sorry!
Wait! Come back!

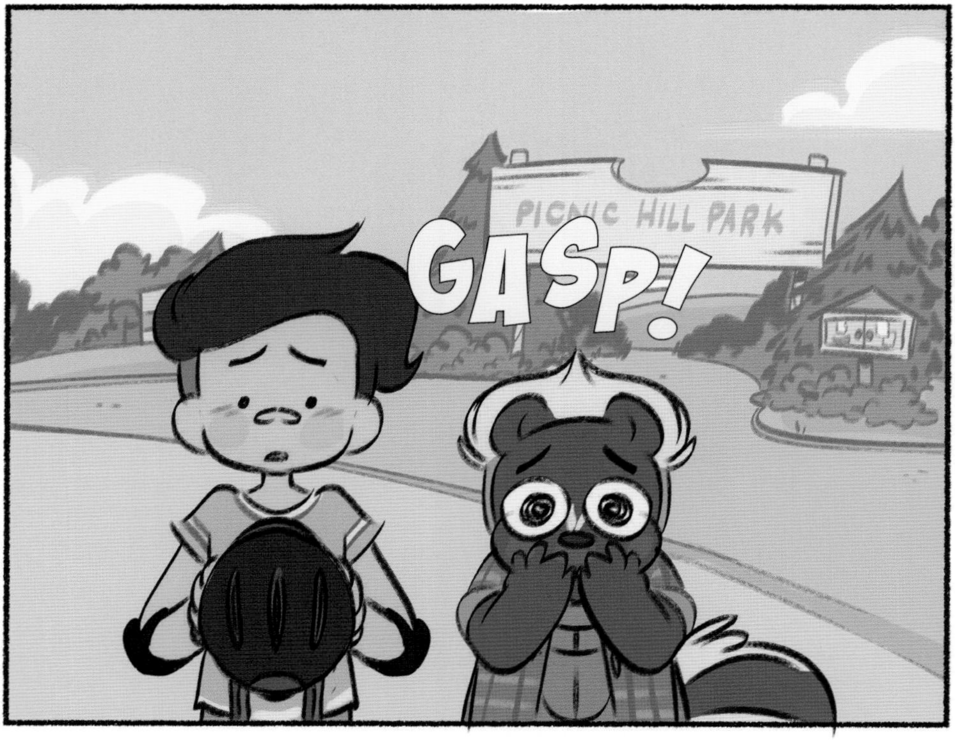
PICNIC HILL PARK
GASP!

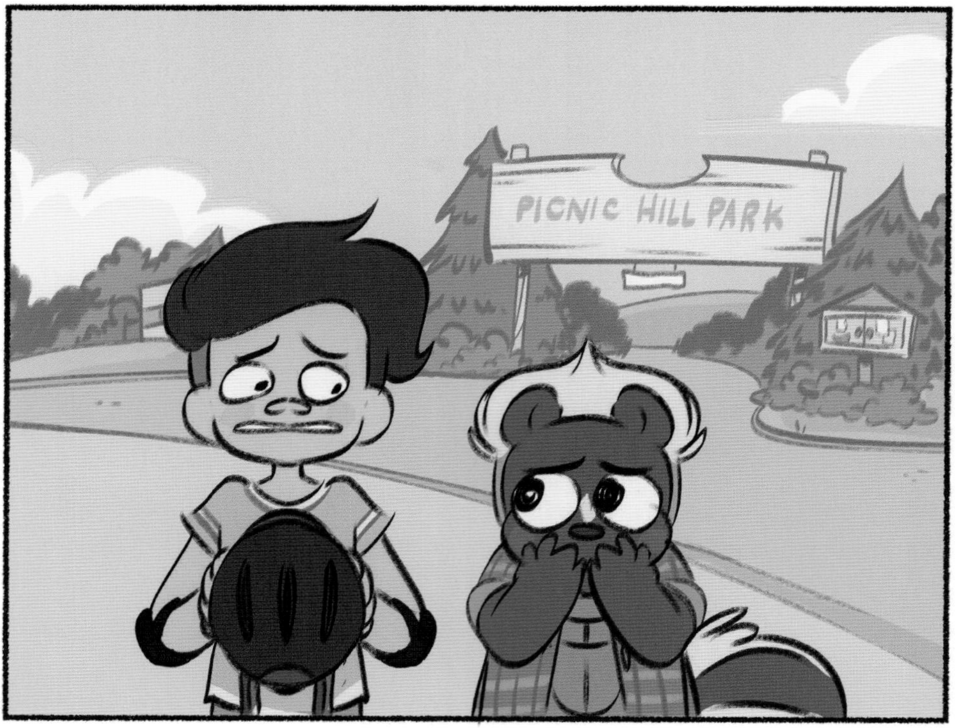
PICNIC HILL PARK

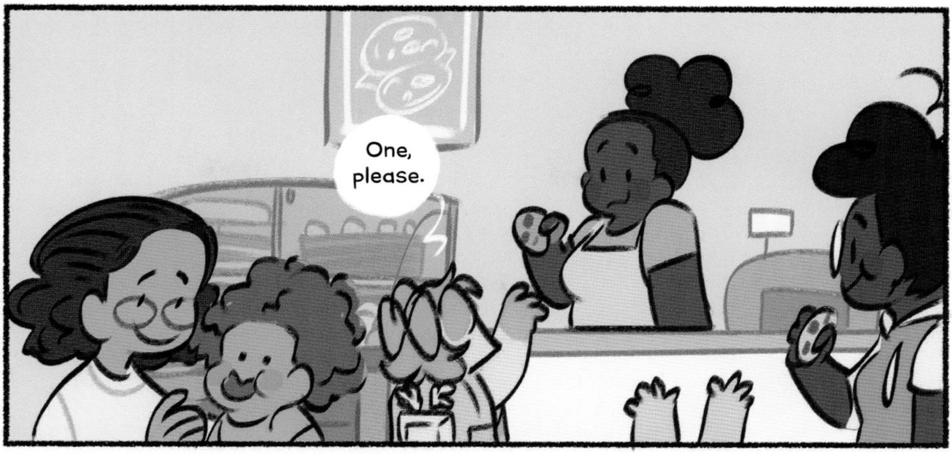
One, please.

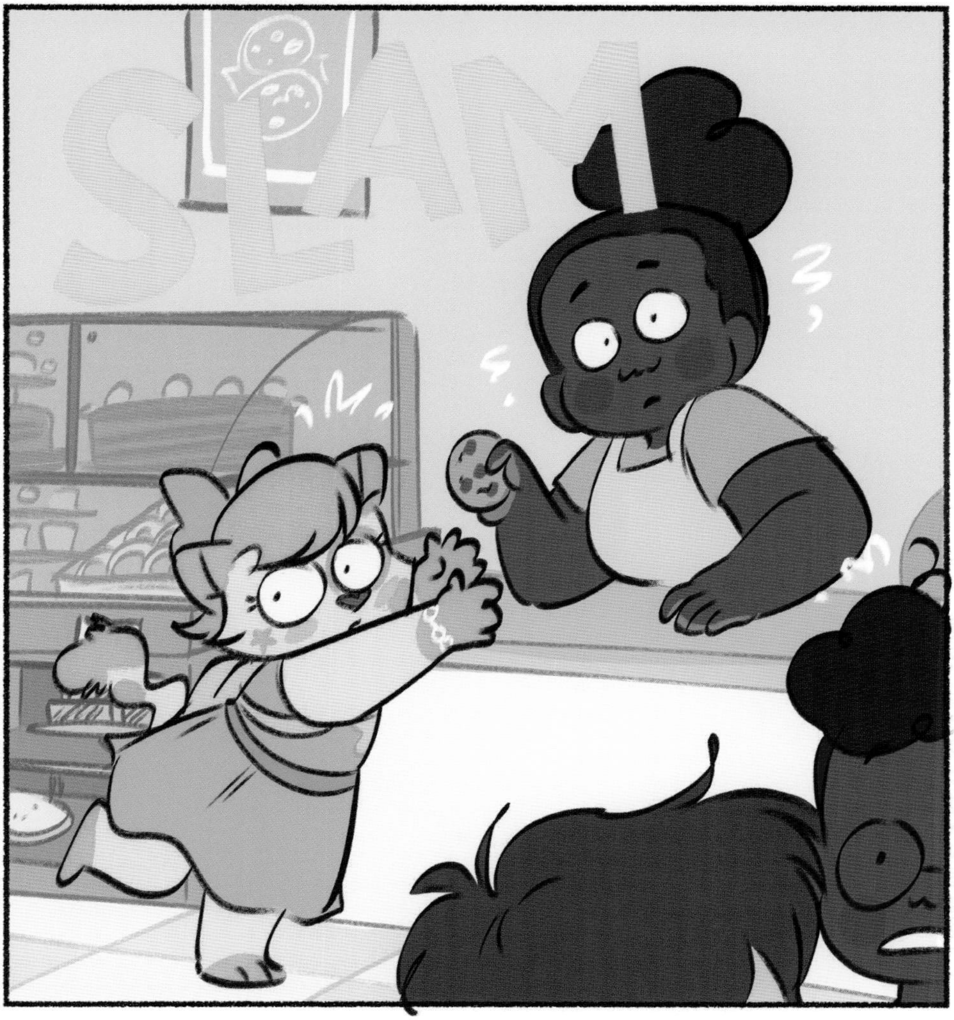
SLAM

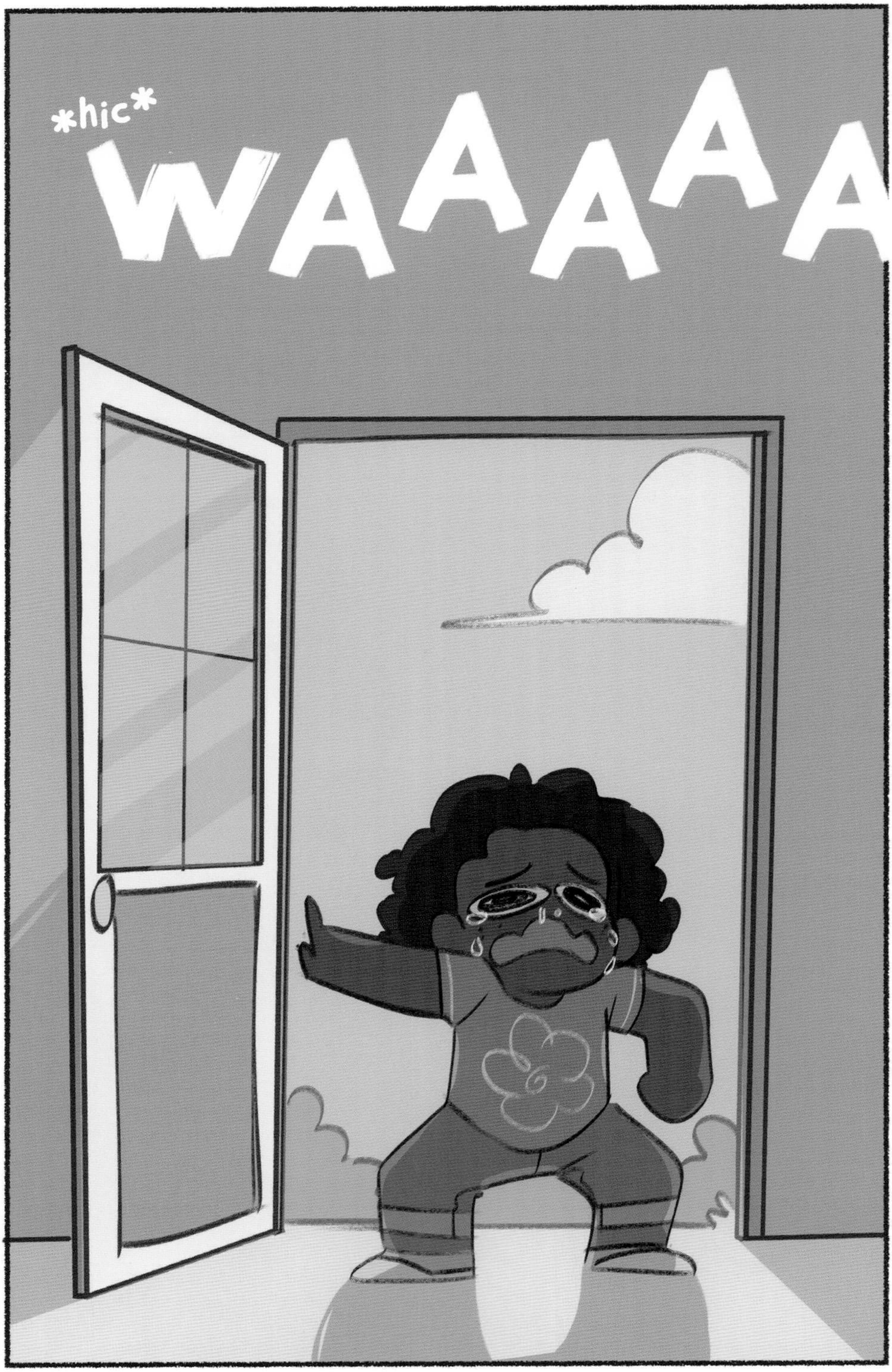
hic
WAAAAAA

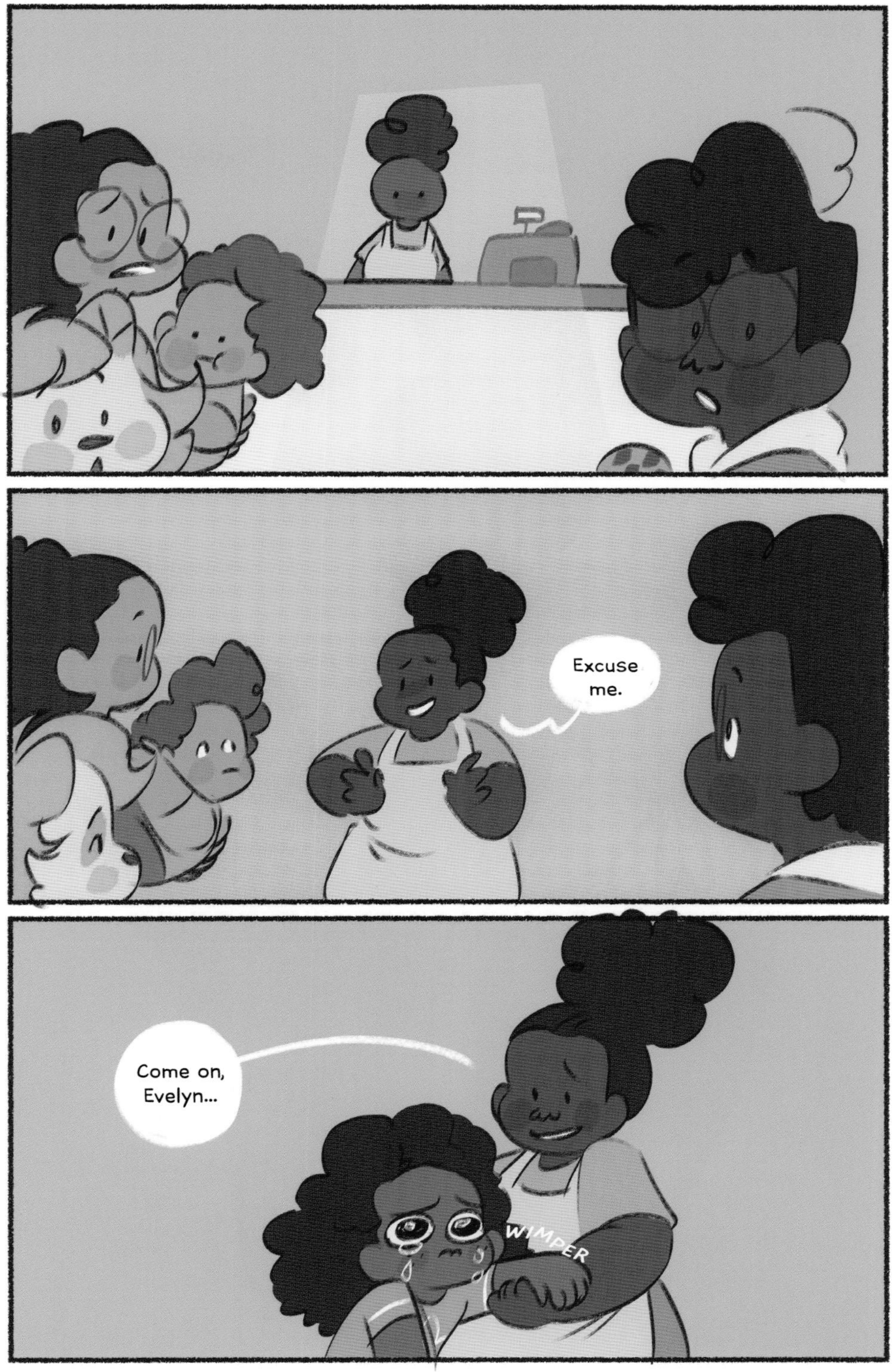
Excuse me.
Come on, Evelyn...
WIMPER

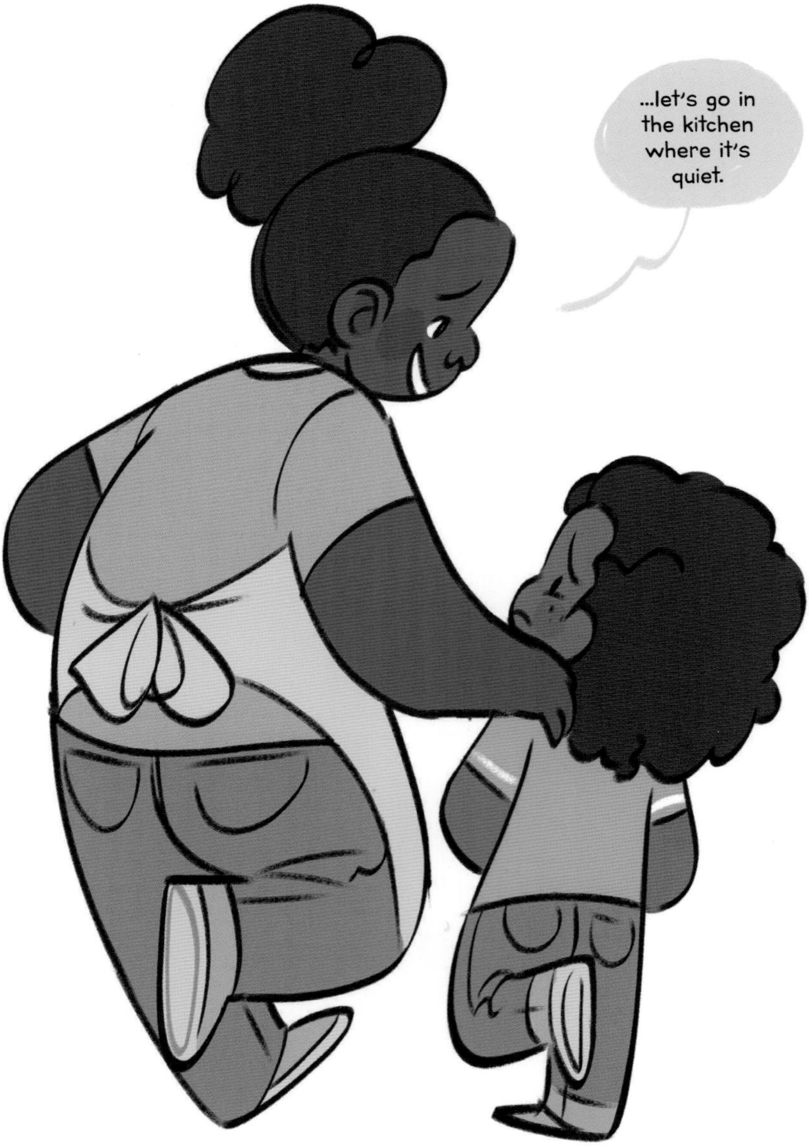
...let's go in the kitchen where it's quiet.

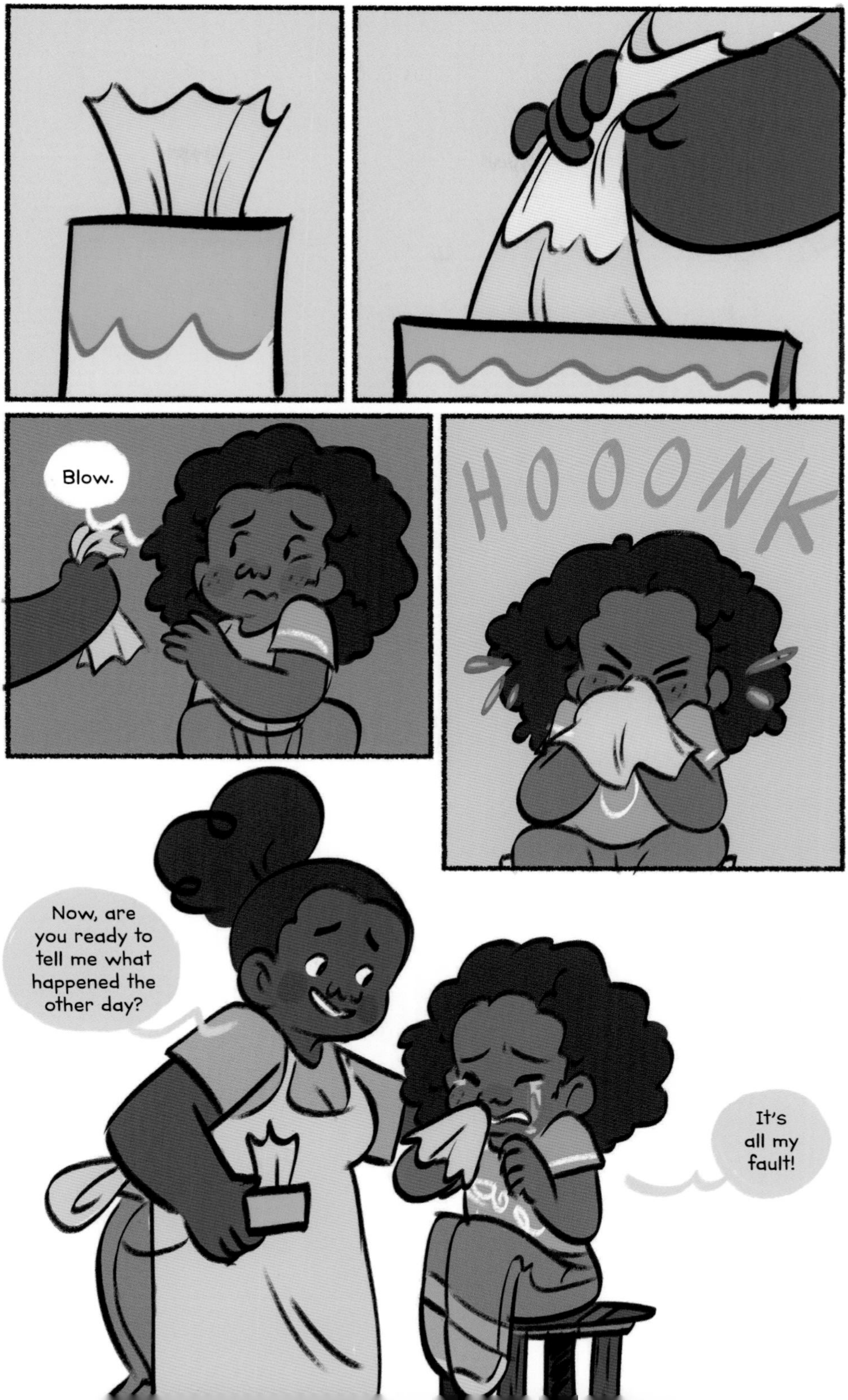
Blow.
HOOONK
Now, are you ready to tell me what happened the other day?
It's all my fault!

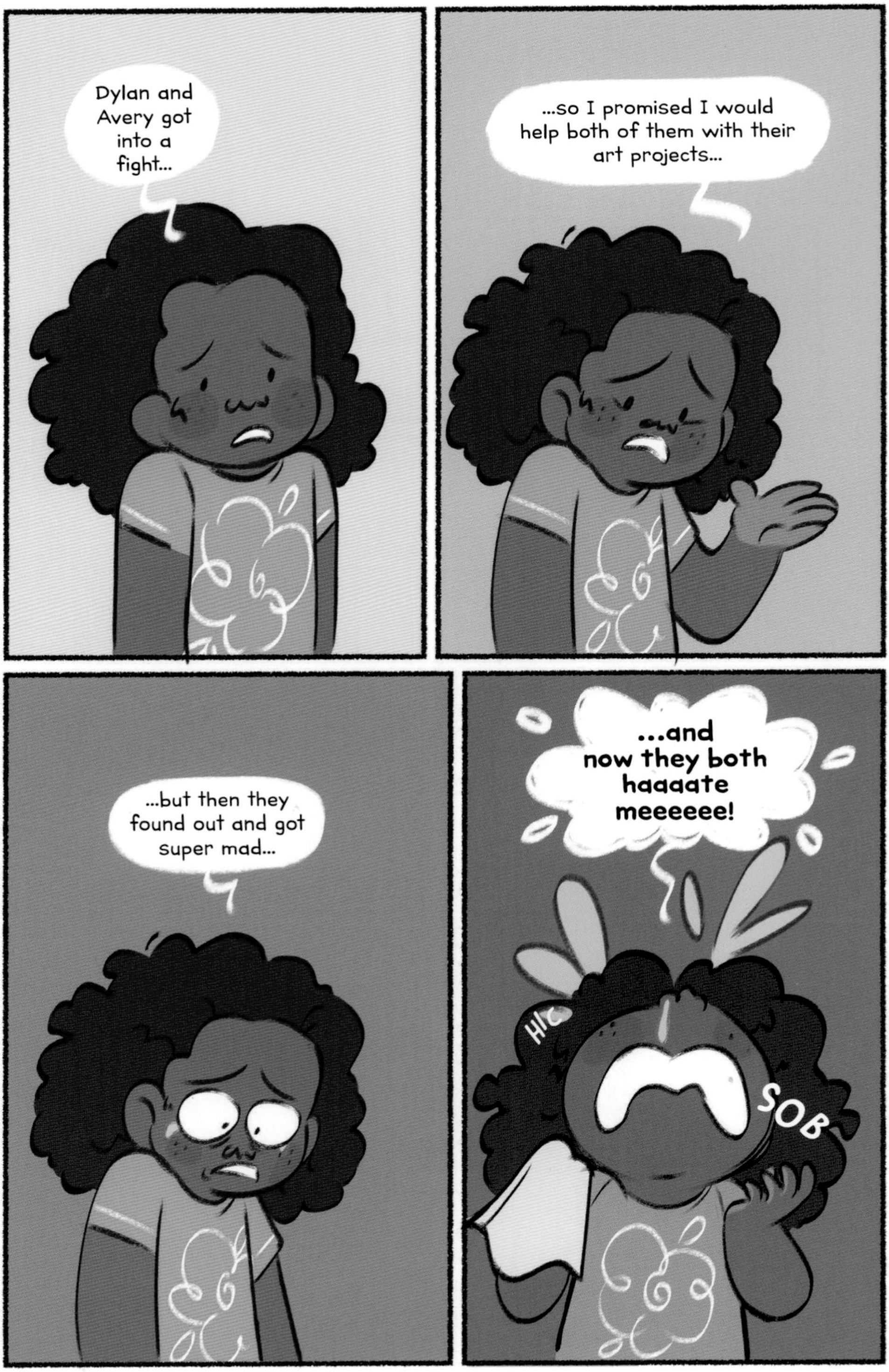
Dylan and Avery got into a fight...
...so I promised I would help both of them with their art projects...
...but then they found out and got super mad...
...and now they both haaaate meeeeee!
HIC
SOB

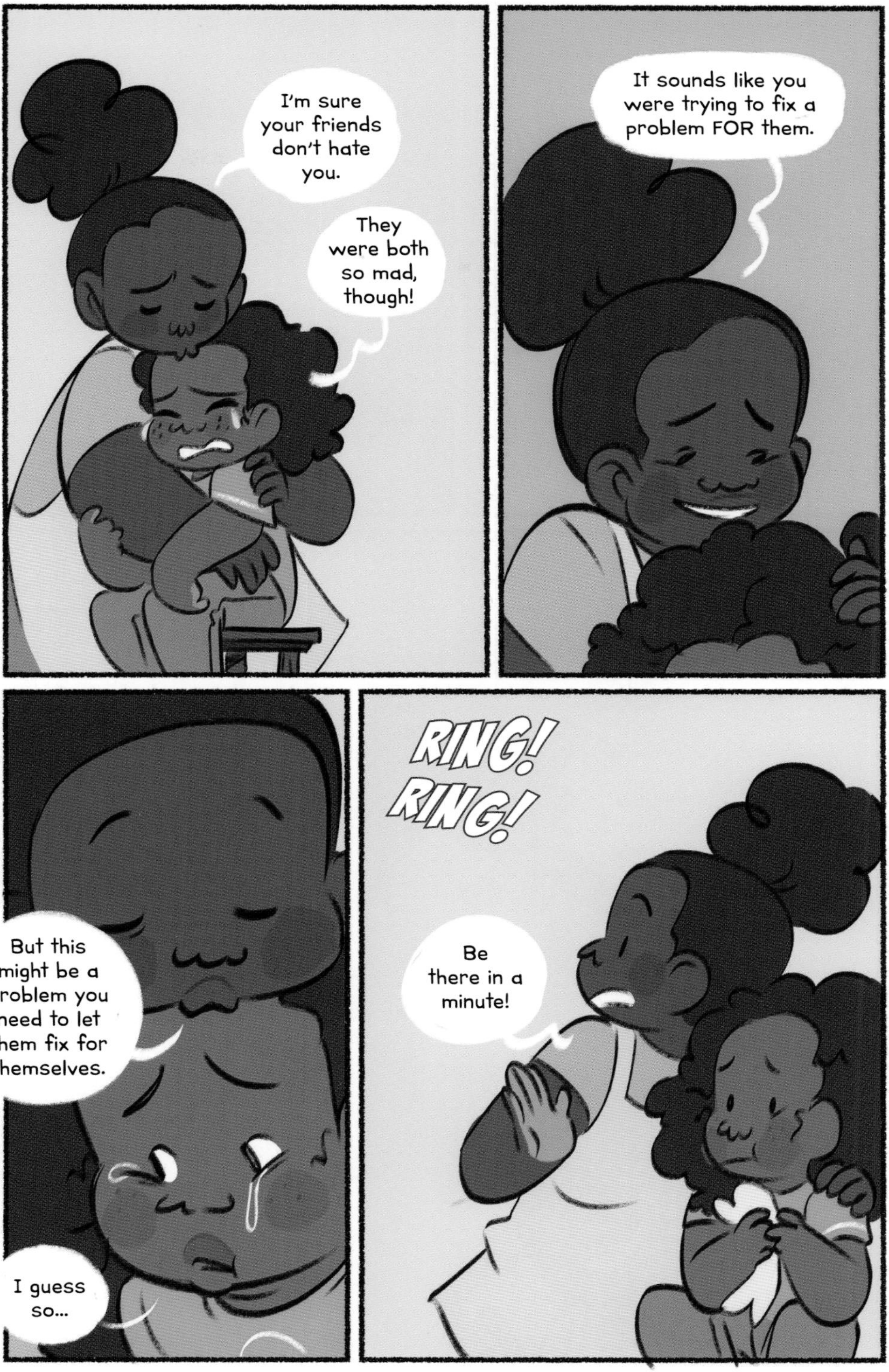
I'm sure your friends don't hate you.
They were both so mad, though!
It sounds like you were trying to fix a problem FOR them.
But this might be a problem you need to let them fix for themselves.
I guess so...
RING! RING!
Be there in a minute!

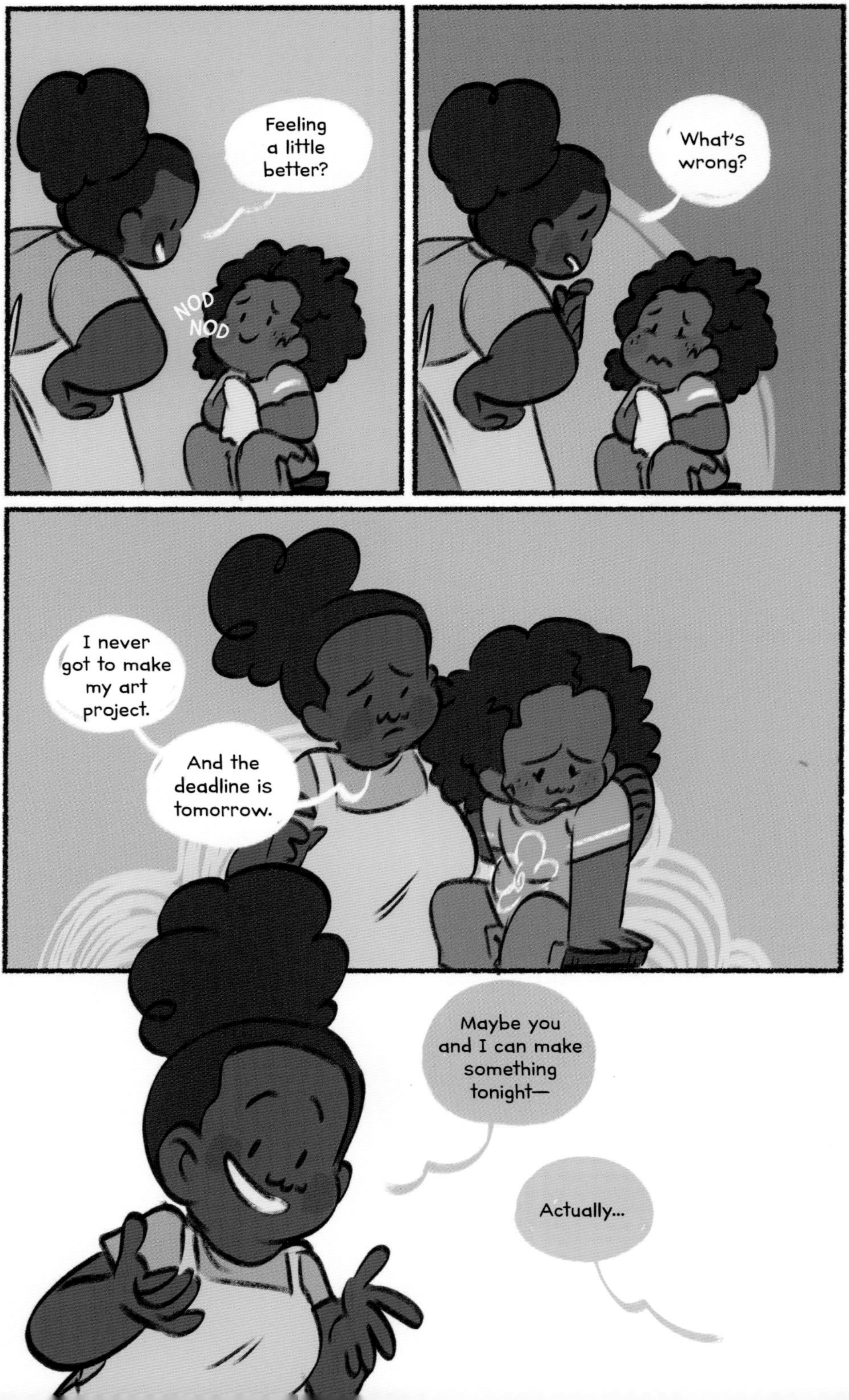

Feeling a little better?
NOD NOD
What's wrong?
I never got to make my art project.
And the deadline is tomorrow.
Maybe you and I can make something tonight—
Actually...

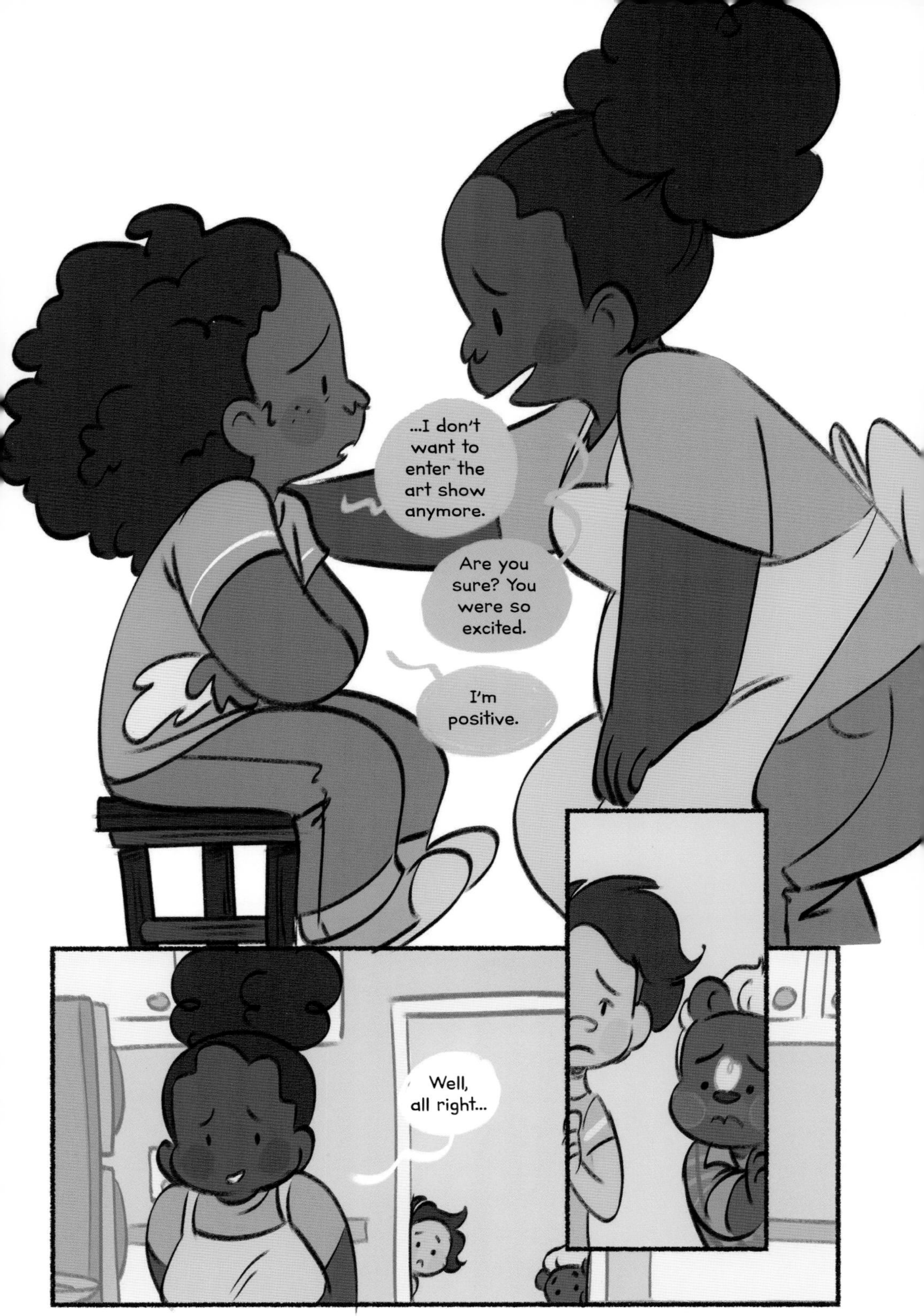
...I don't want to enter the art show anymore.
Are you sure? You were so excited.
I'm positive.
Well, all right...

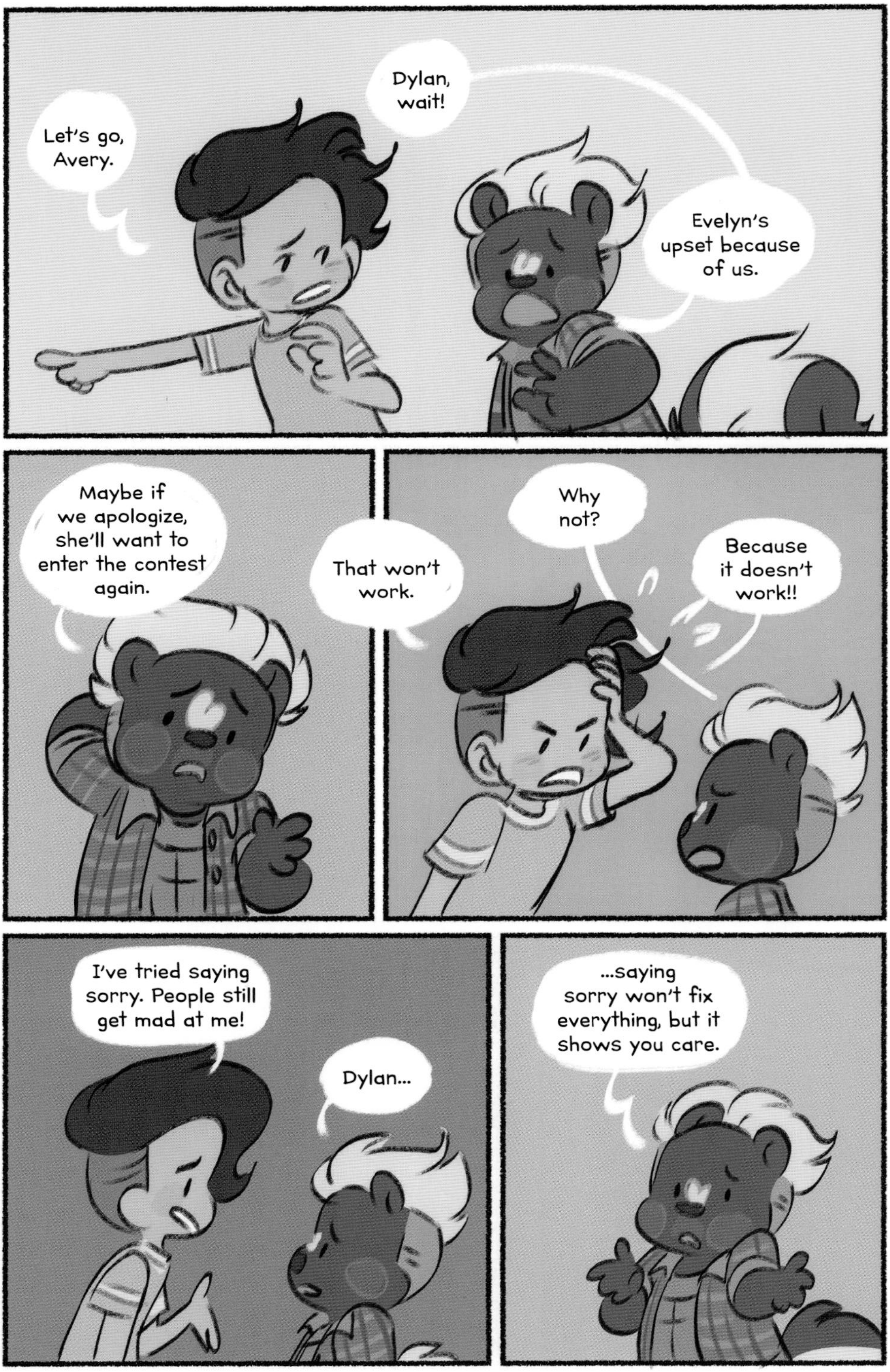
Let's go, Avery.
Dylan, wait!
Evelyn's upset because of us.
Maybe if we apologize, she'll want to enter the contest again.
That won't work.
Why not?
Because it doesn't work!!
I've tried saying sorry. People still get mad at me!
Dylan...
...saying sorry won't fix everything, but it shows you care.

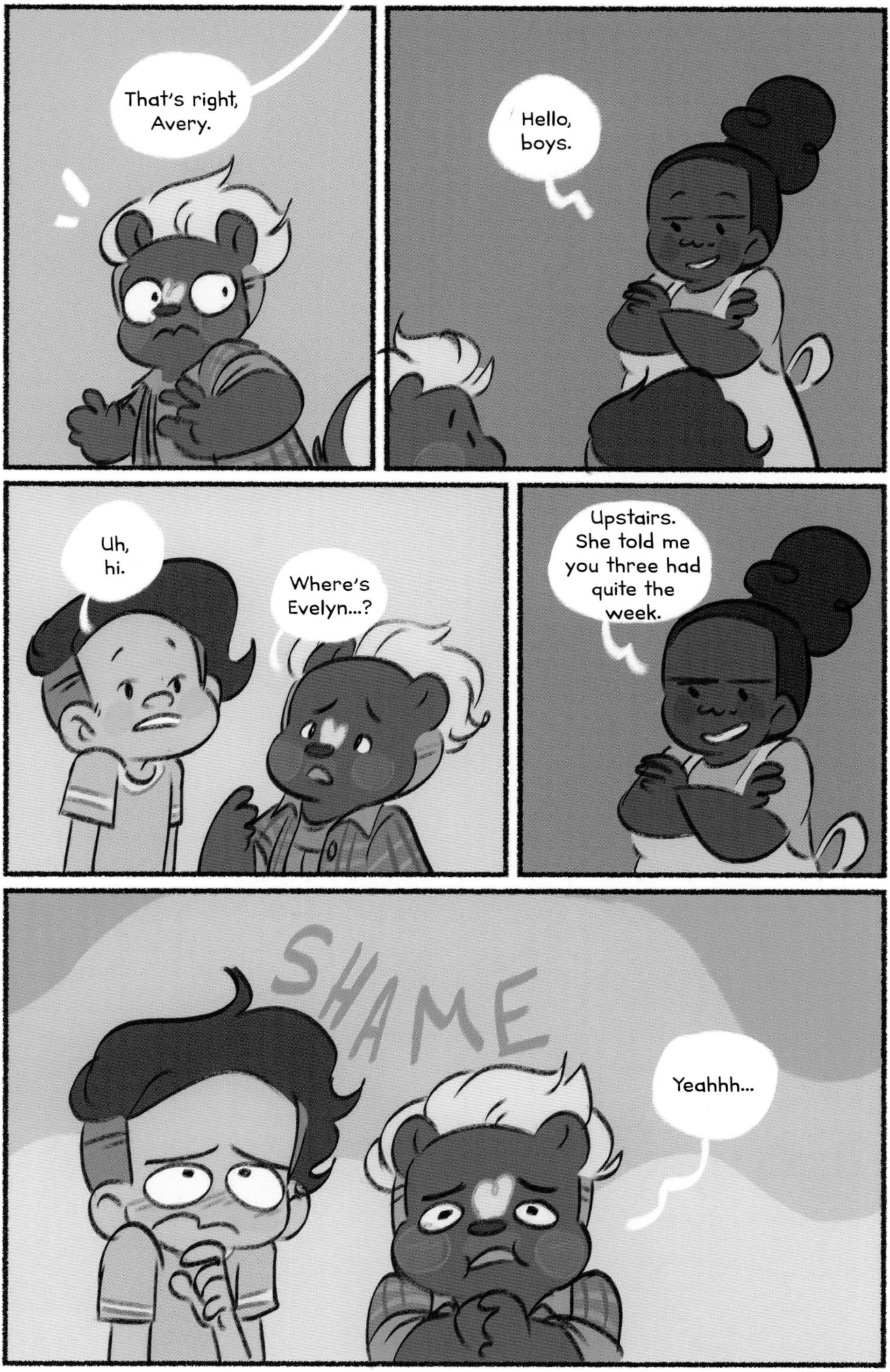
That's right, Avery.
Hello, boys.
Uh, hi.
Where's Evelyn...?
Upstairs. She told me you three had quite the week.
SHAME
Yeahhh...

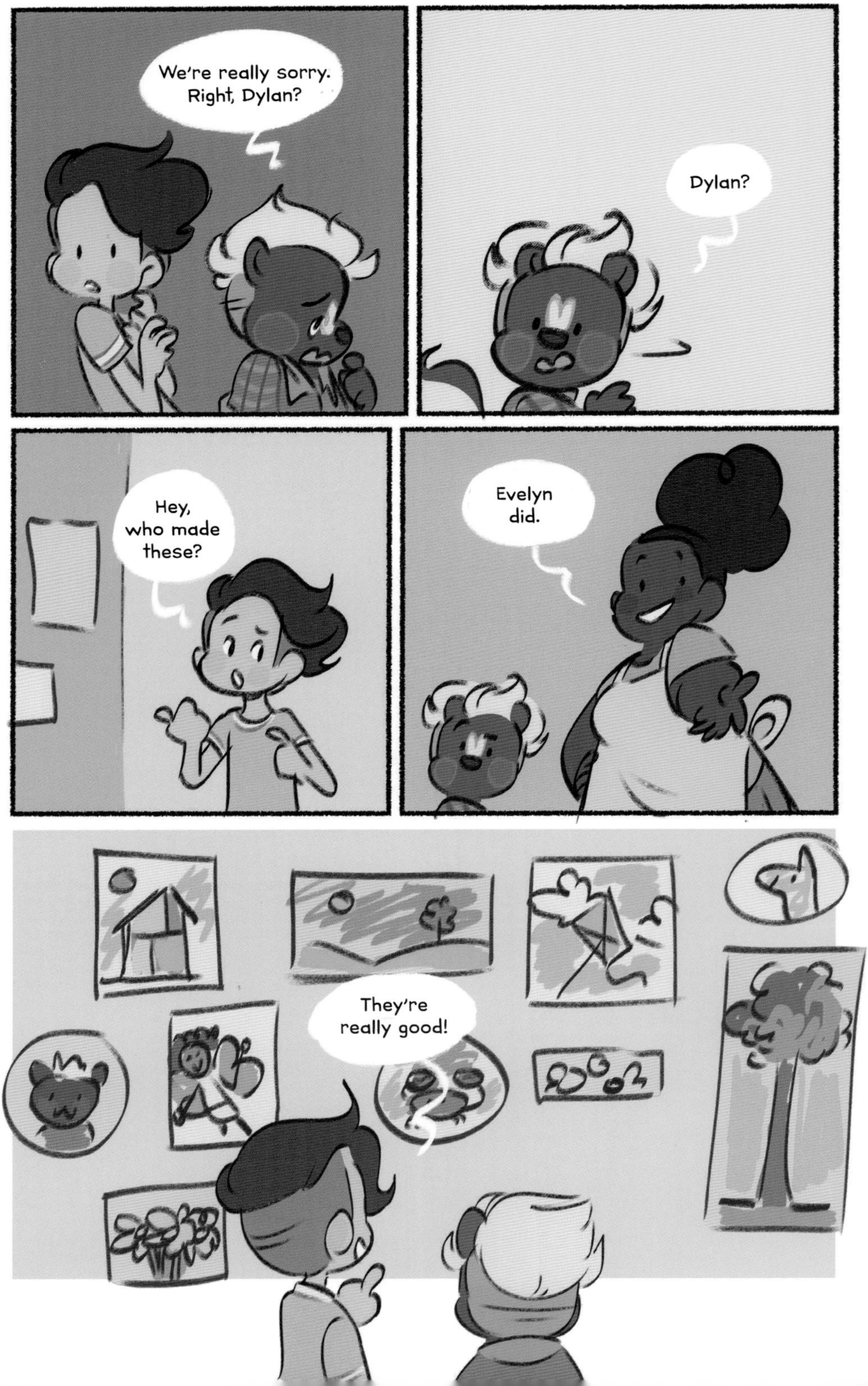
We're really sorry.
Right, Dylan?
Dylan?
Hey,
who made
these?
Evelyn
did.
They're
really good!

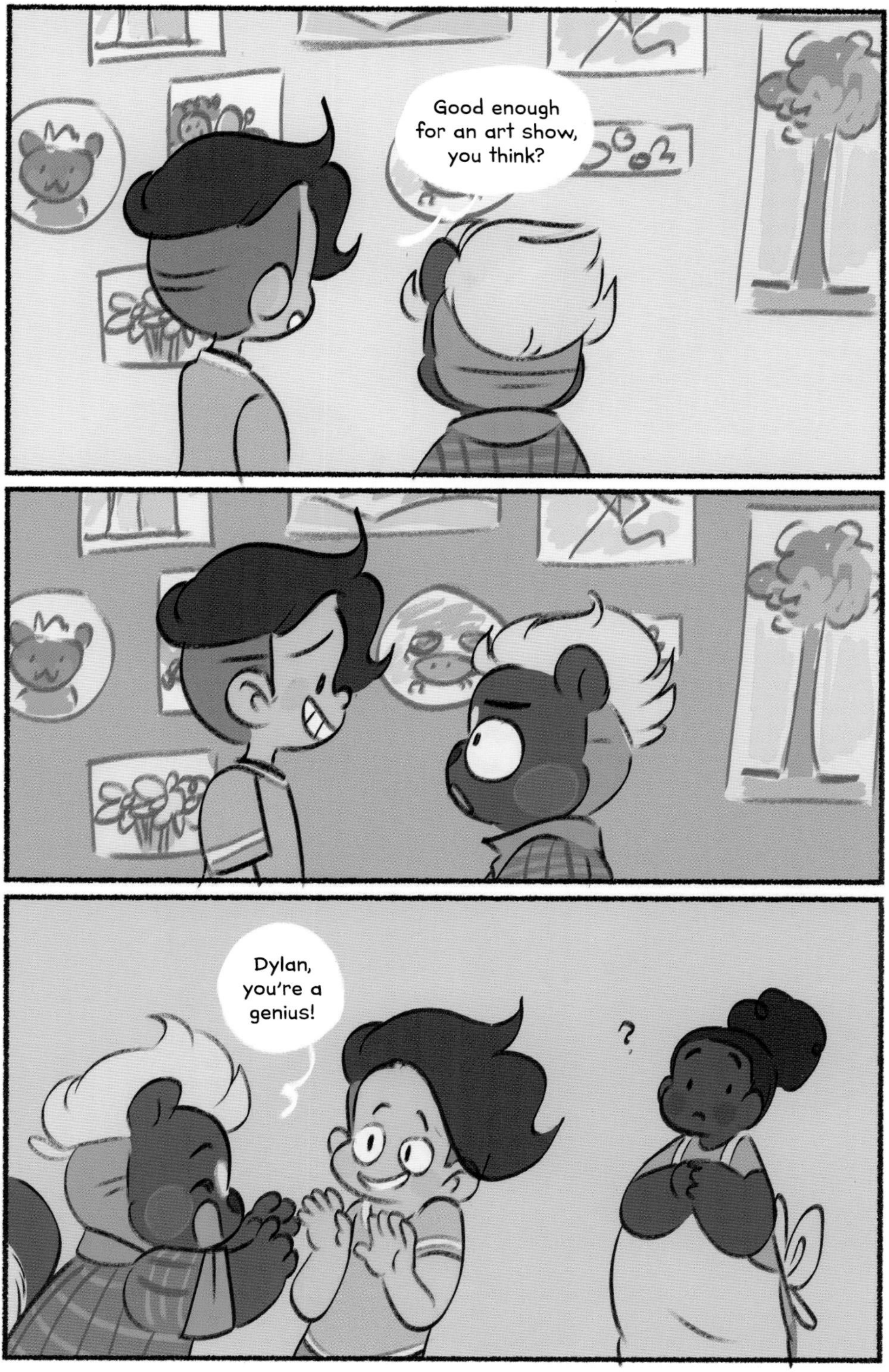
Good enough for an art show, you think?
Dylan, you're a genius!
?

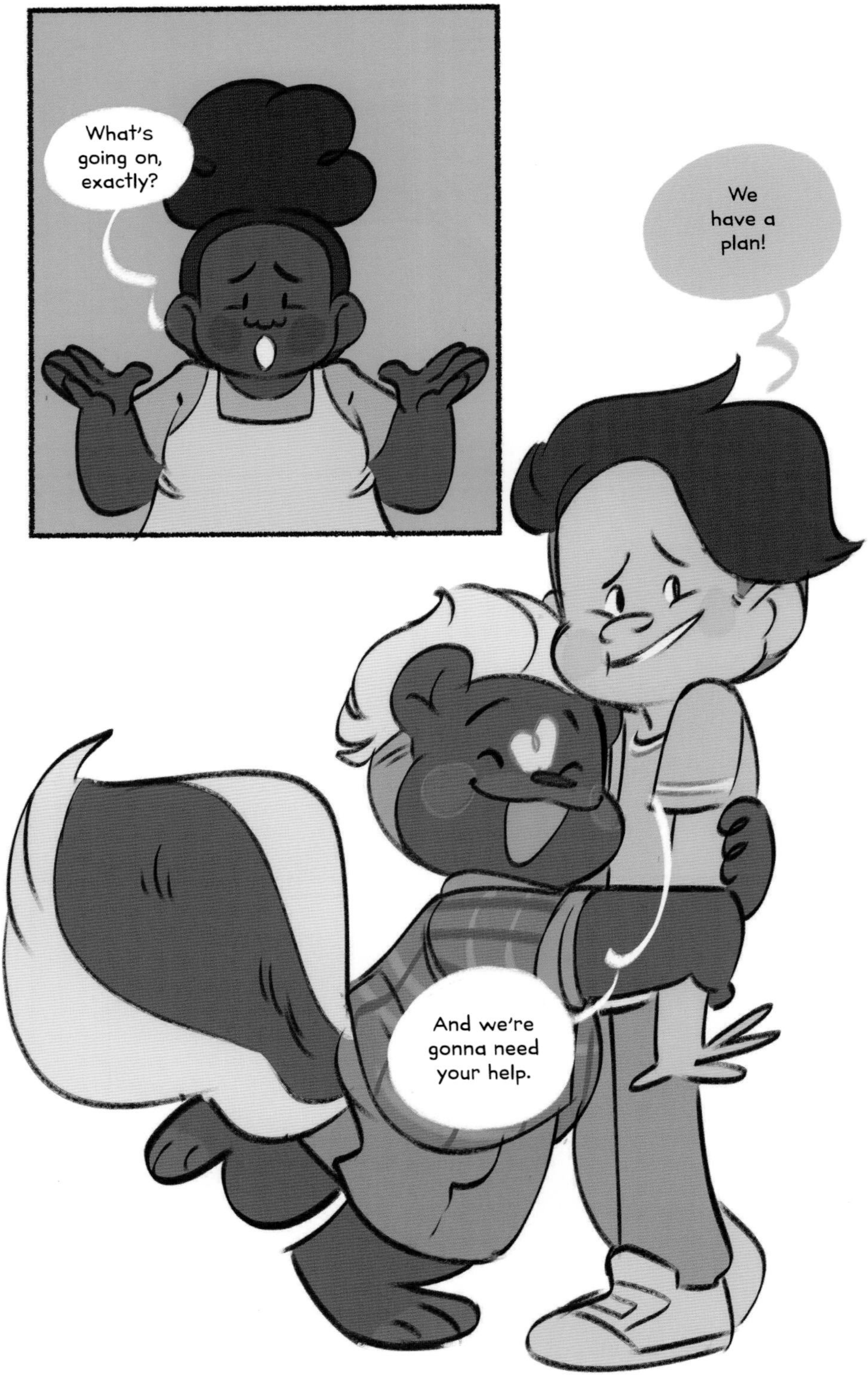
What's going on, exactly?
We have a plan!
And we're gonna need your help.

CHAPTER 4

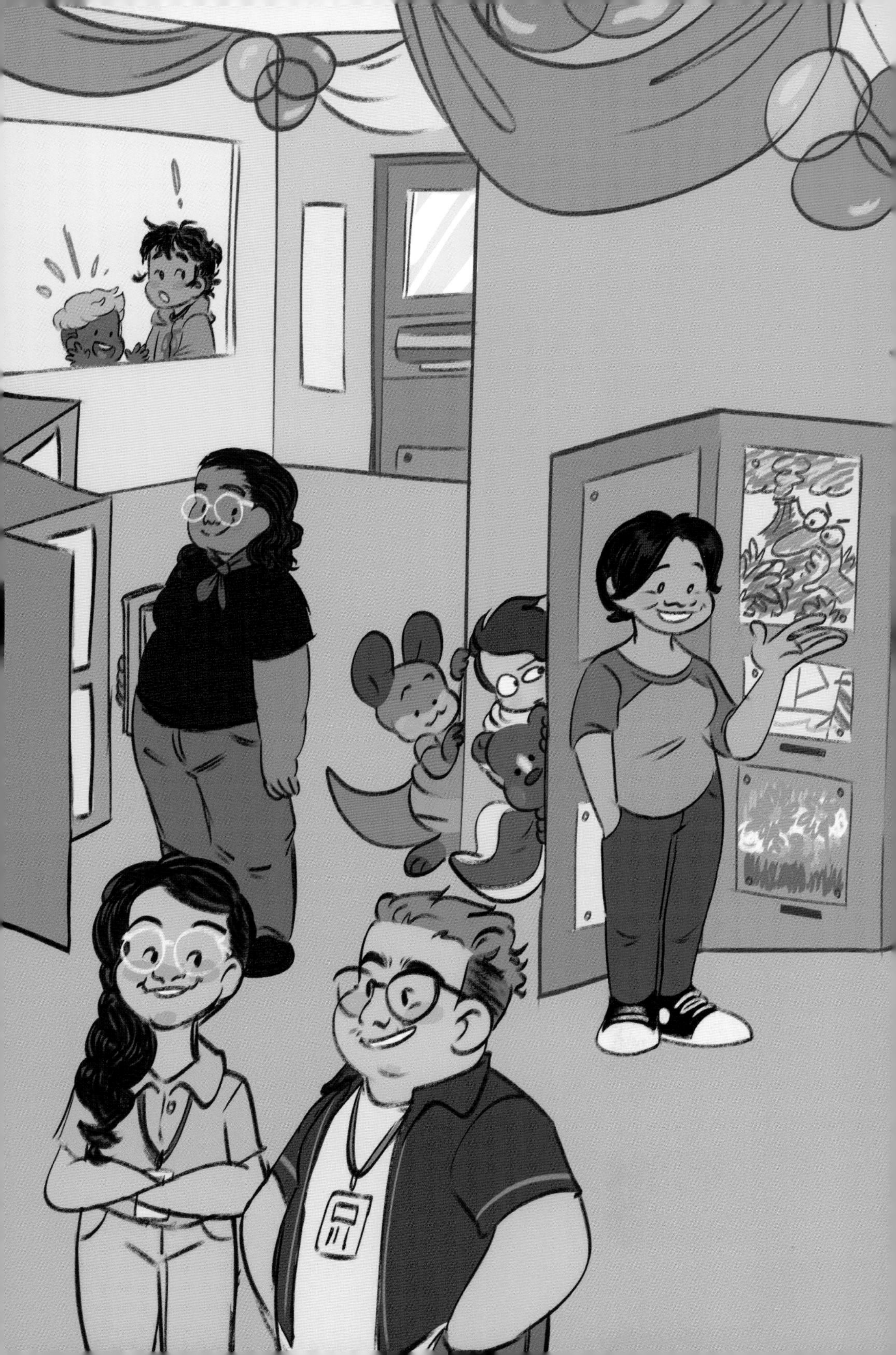

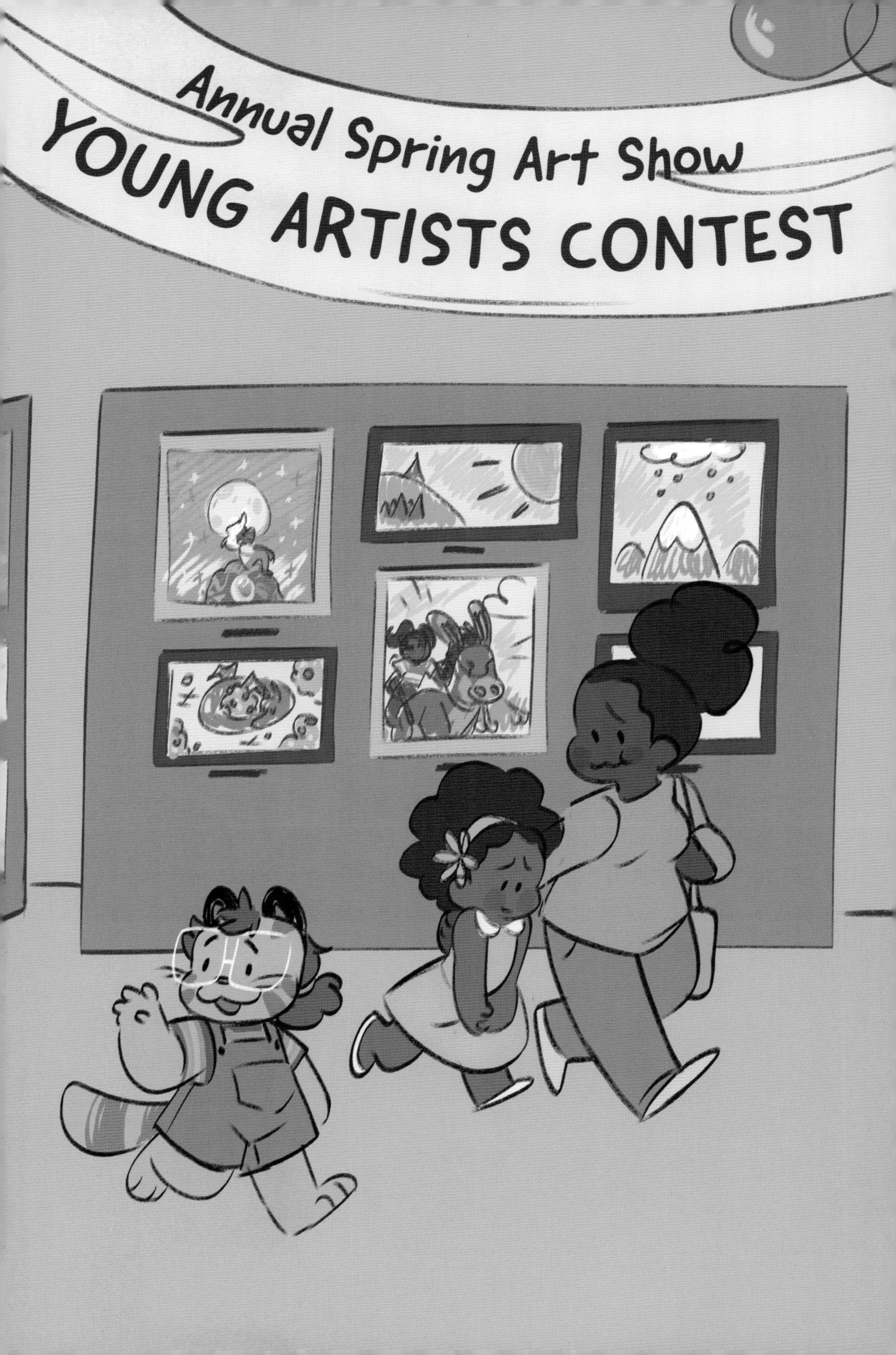
Annual Spring Art Show
YOUNG ARTISTS CONTEST

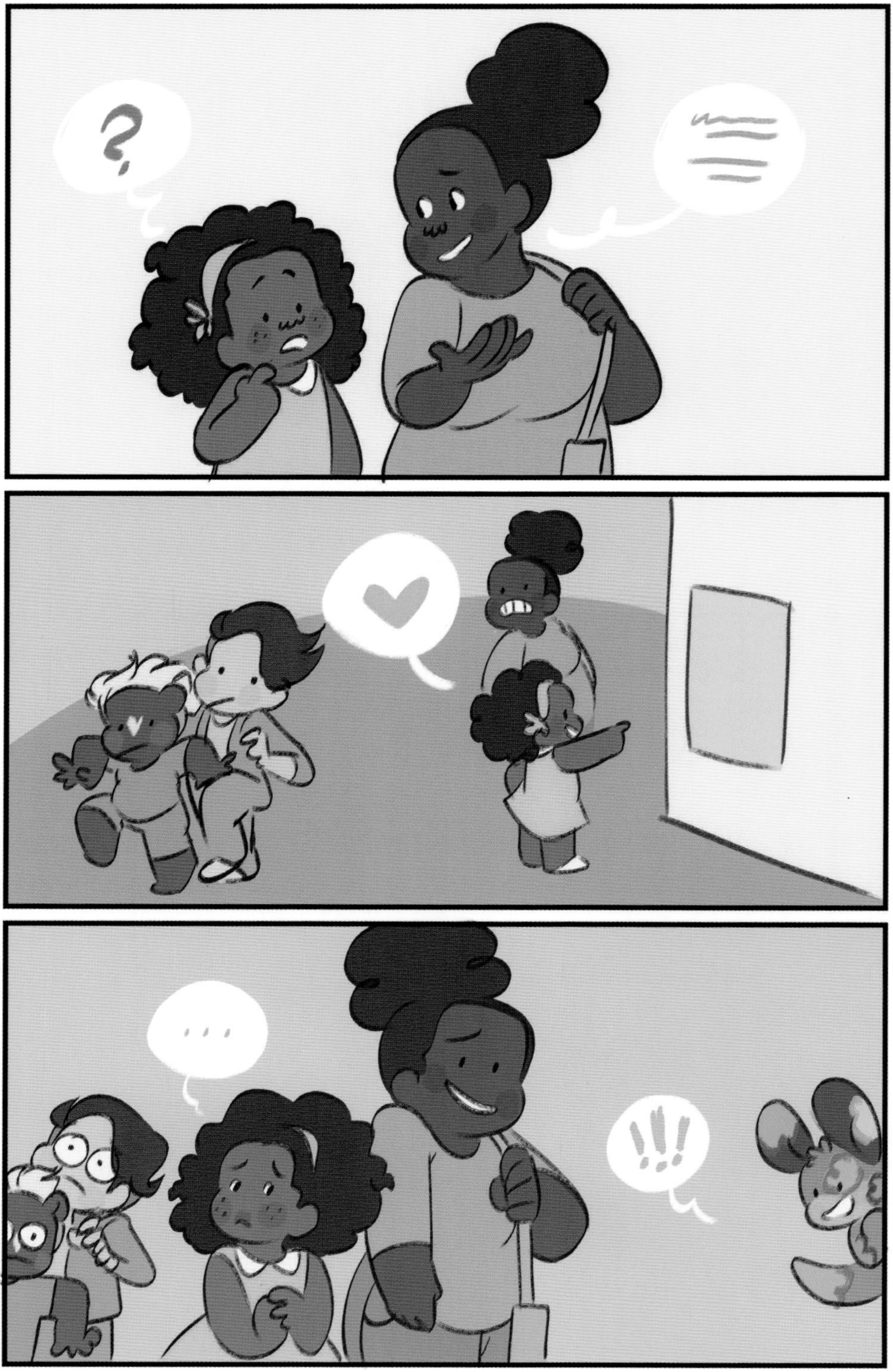
?
...
!!!

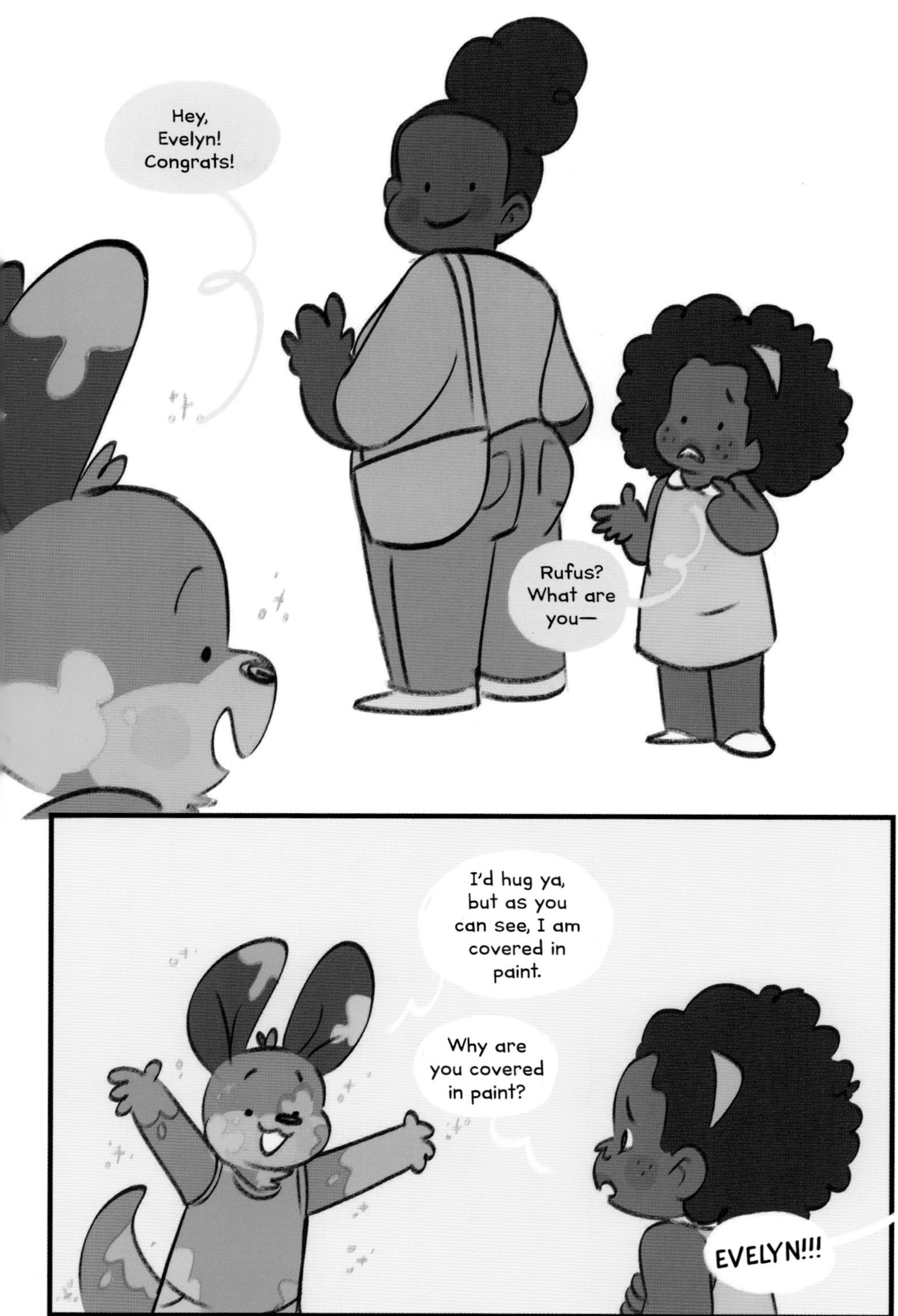
Hey, Evelyn! Congrats!
Rufus? What are you—
I'd hug ya, but as you can see, I am covered in paint.
Why are you covered in paint?
EVELYN!!!

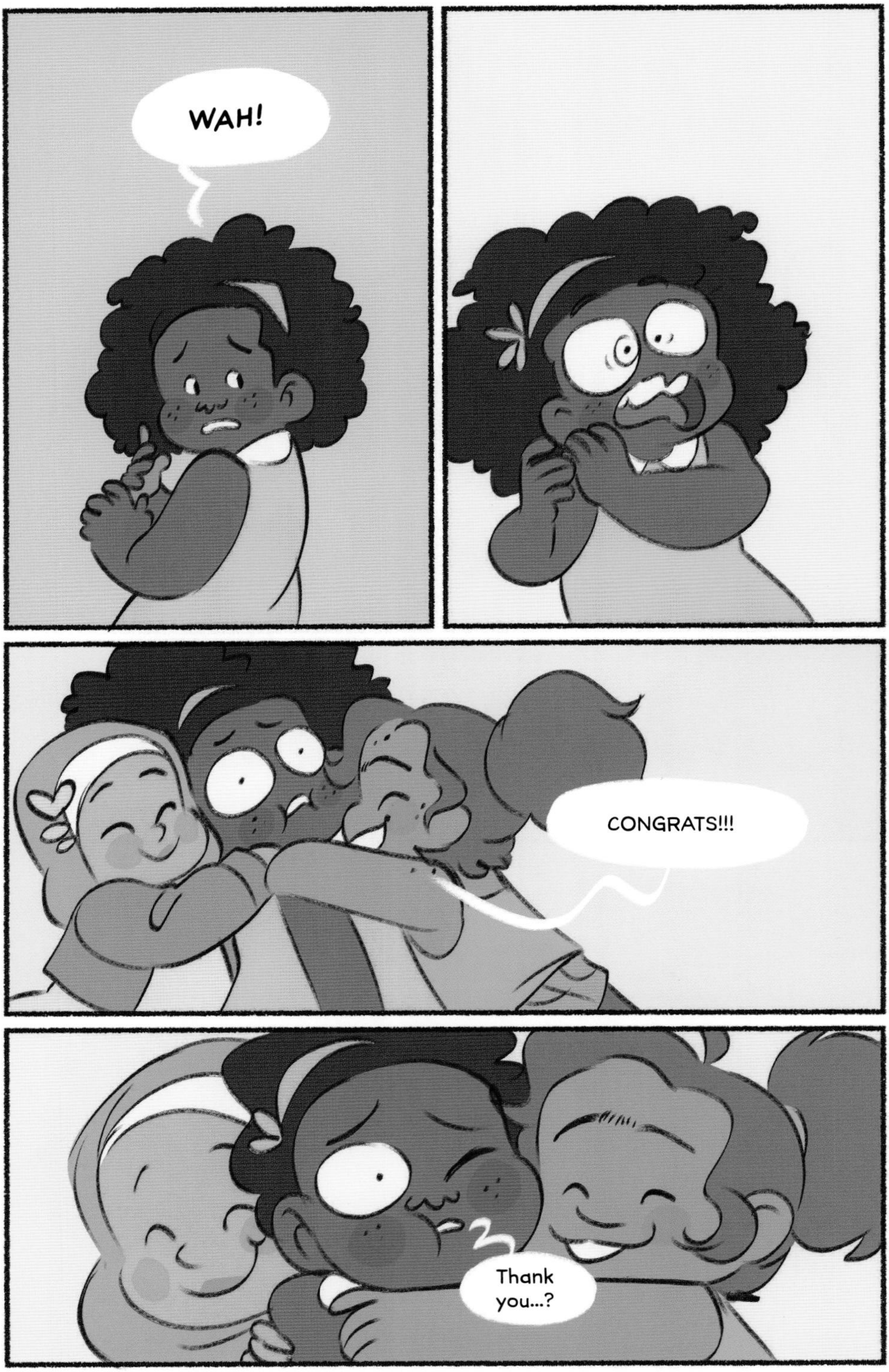
WAH!
CONGRATS!!!
Thank you...?

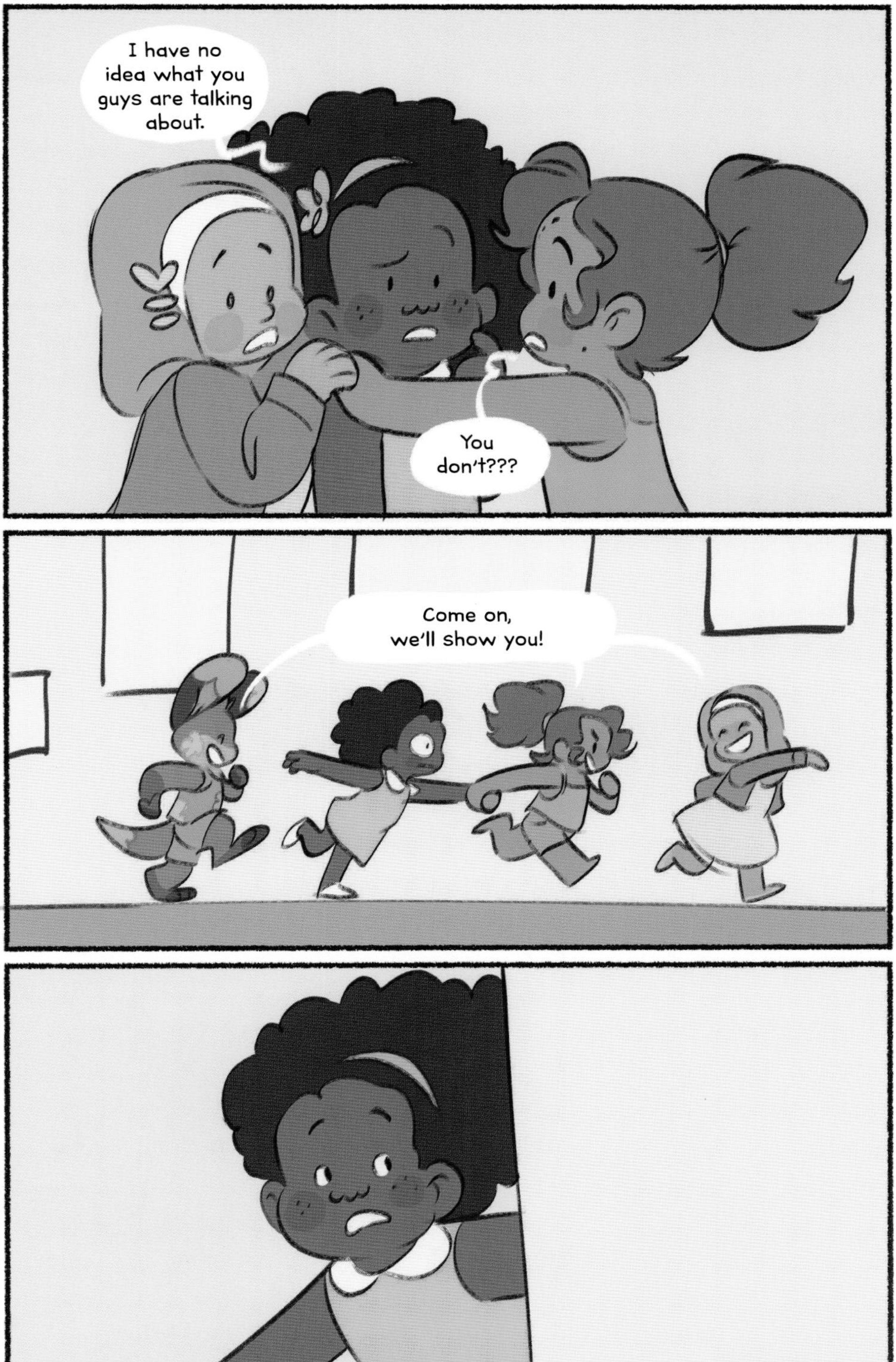
I have no idea what you guys are talking about.
You don't???
Come on, we'll show you!

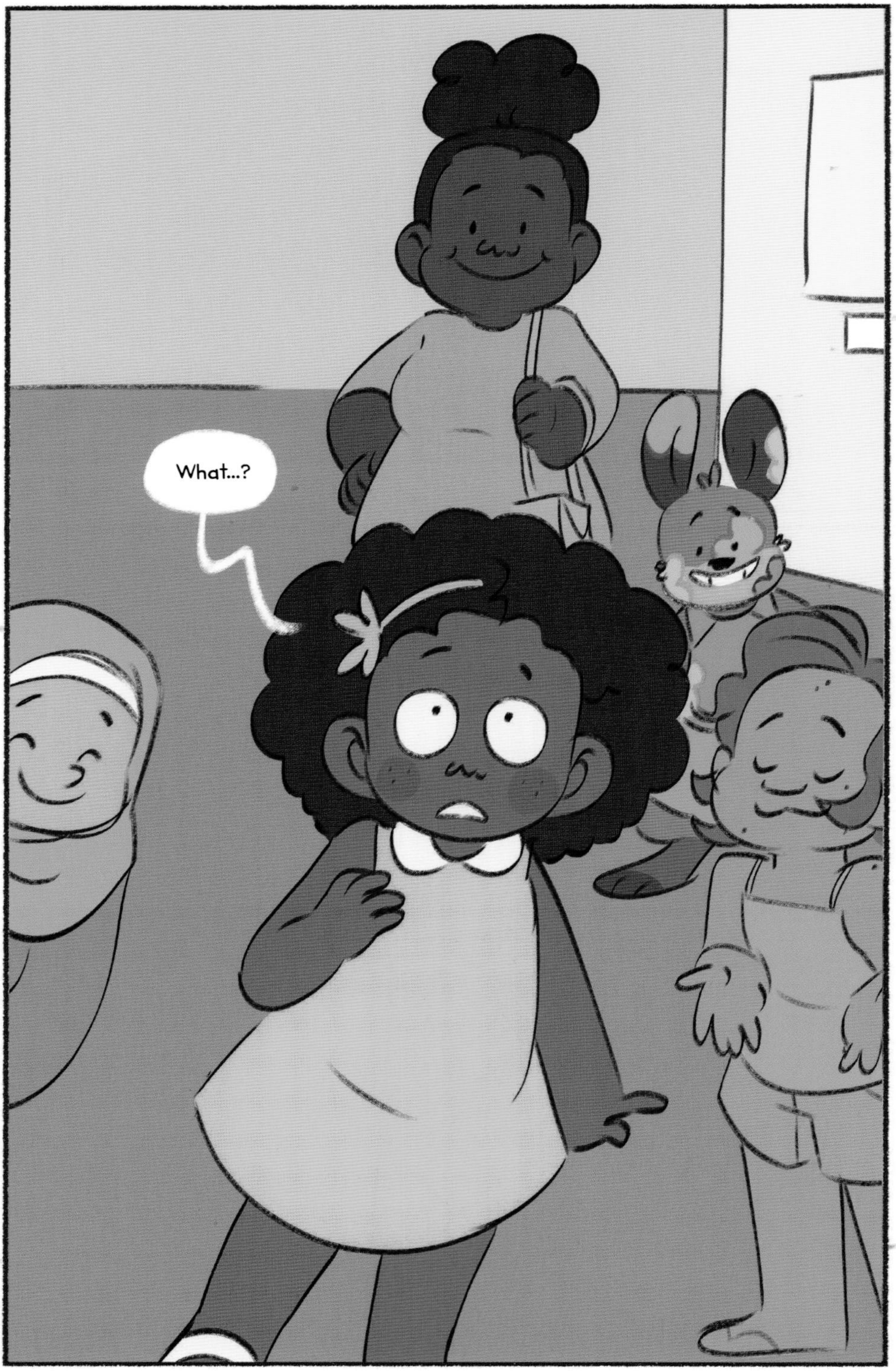
What...?

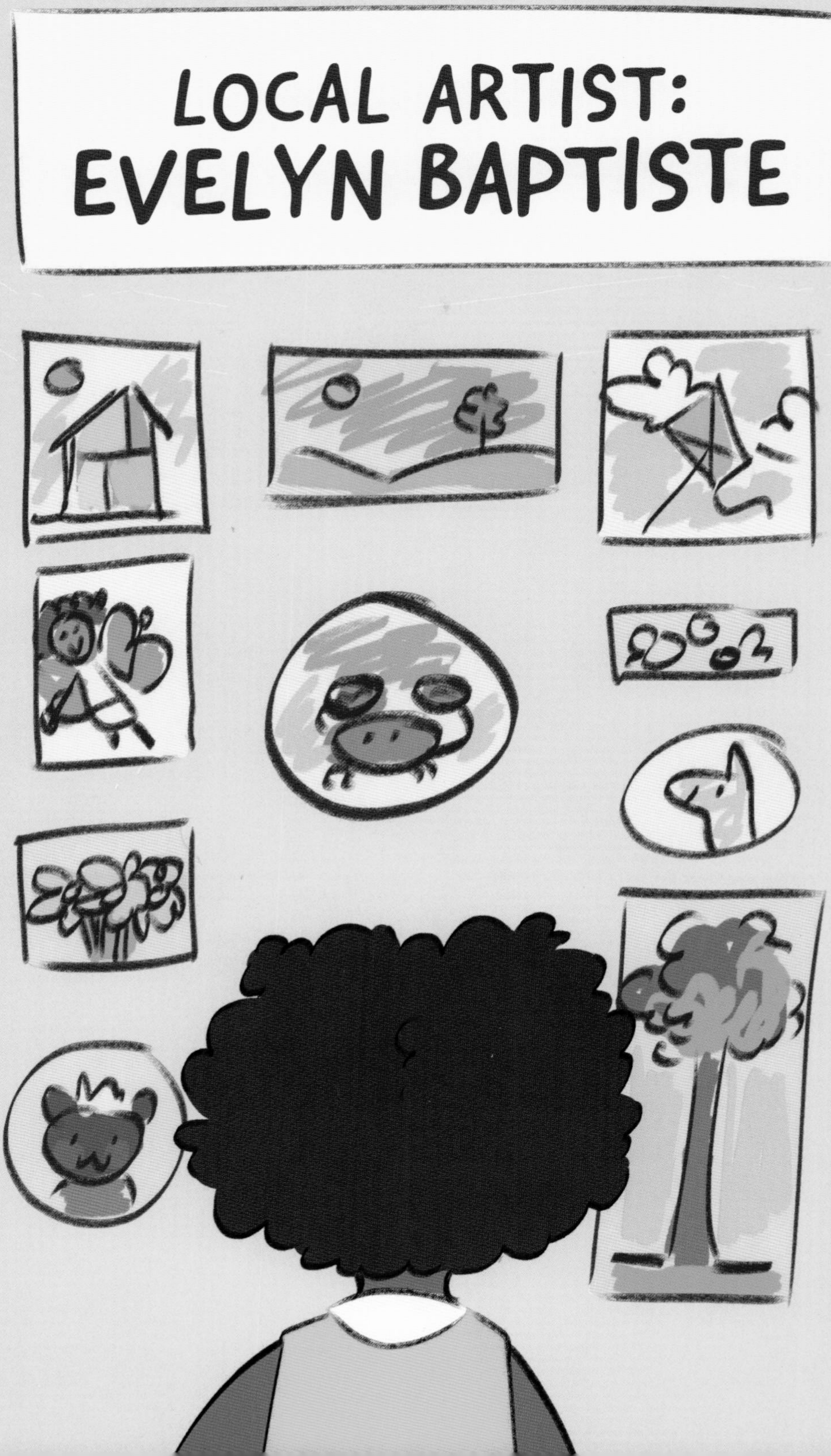
LOCAL ARTIST:
EVELYN BAPTISTE

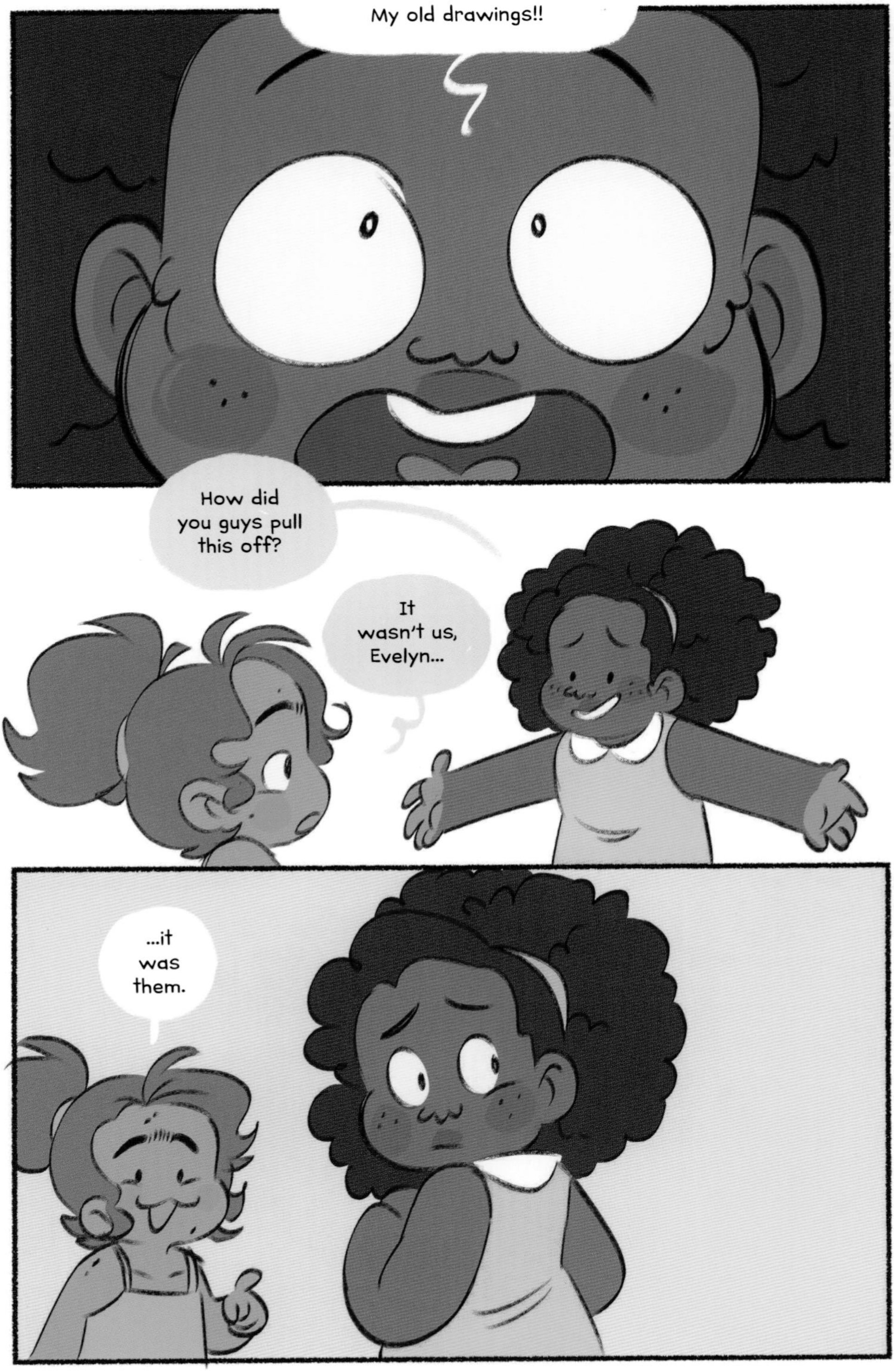
My old drawings!!
How did you guys pull this off?
It wasn't us, Evelyn...
...it was them.

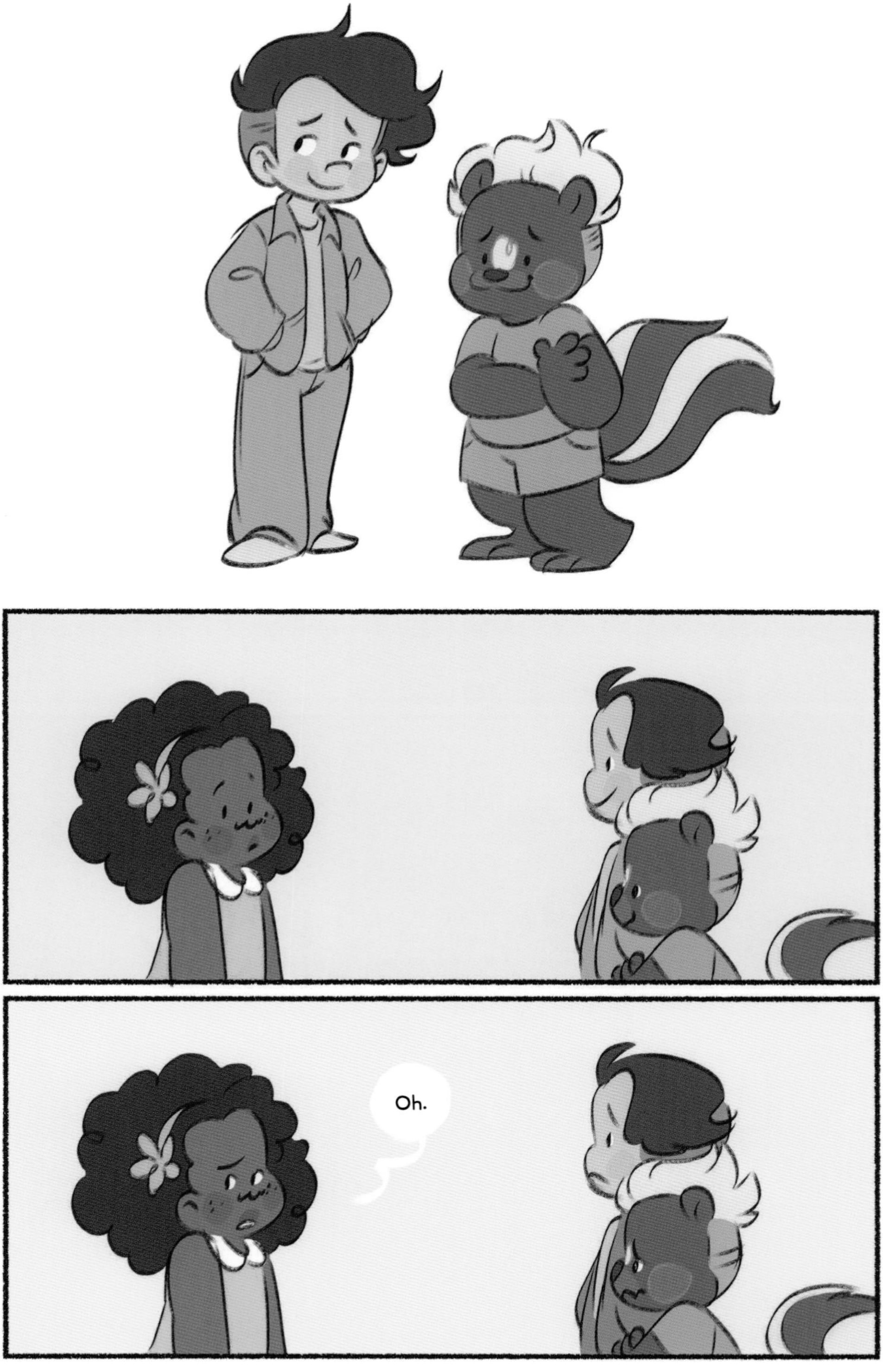
Oh.

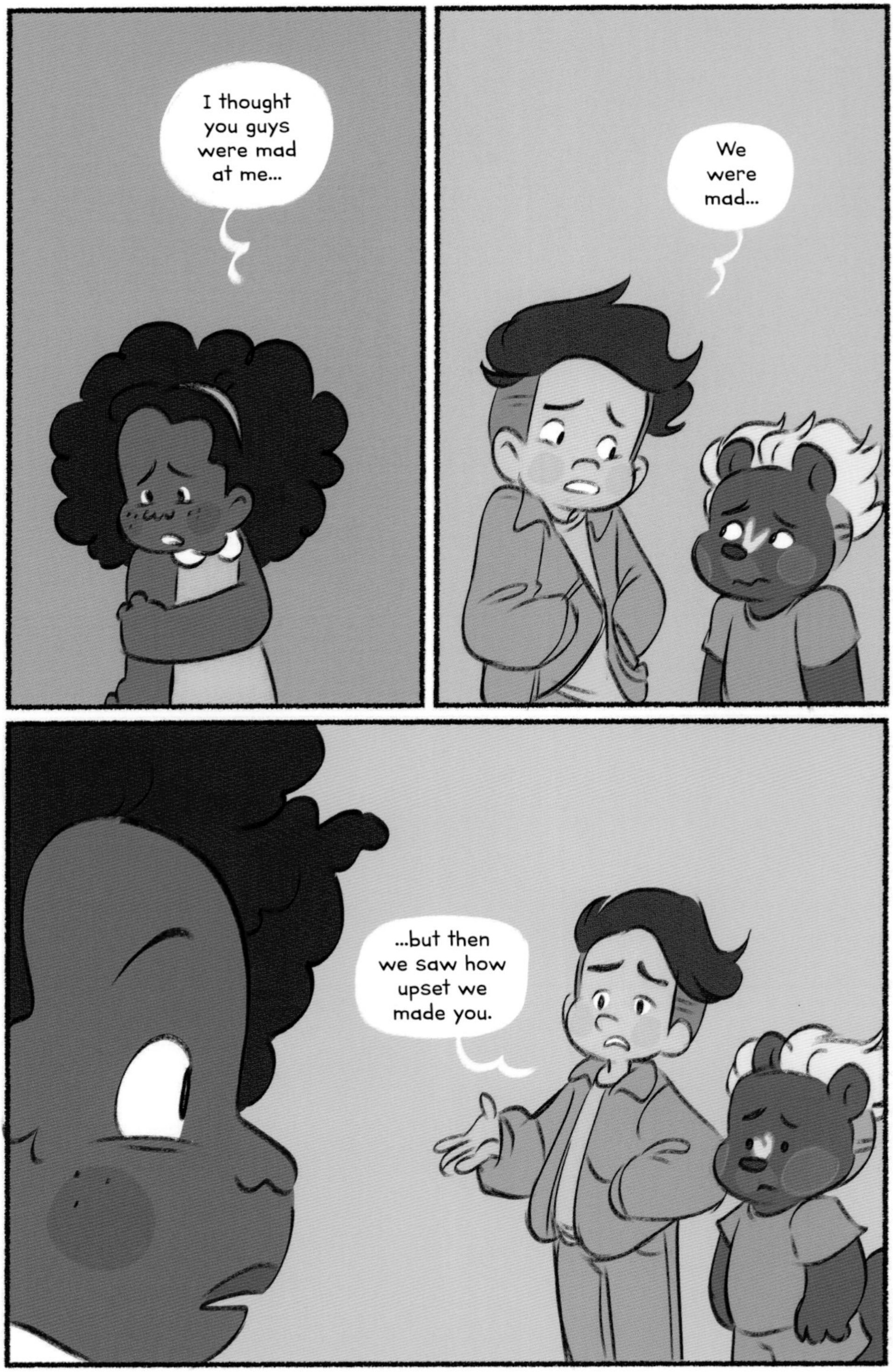
I thought you guys were mad at me...
We were mad...
...but then we saw how upset we made you.

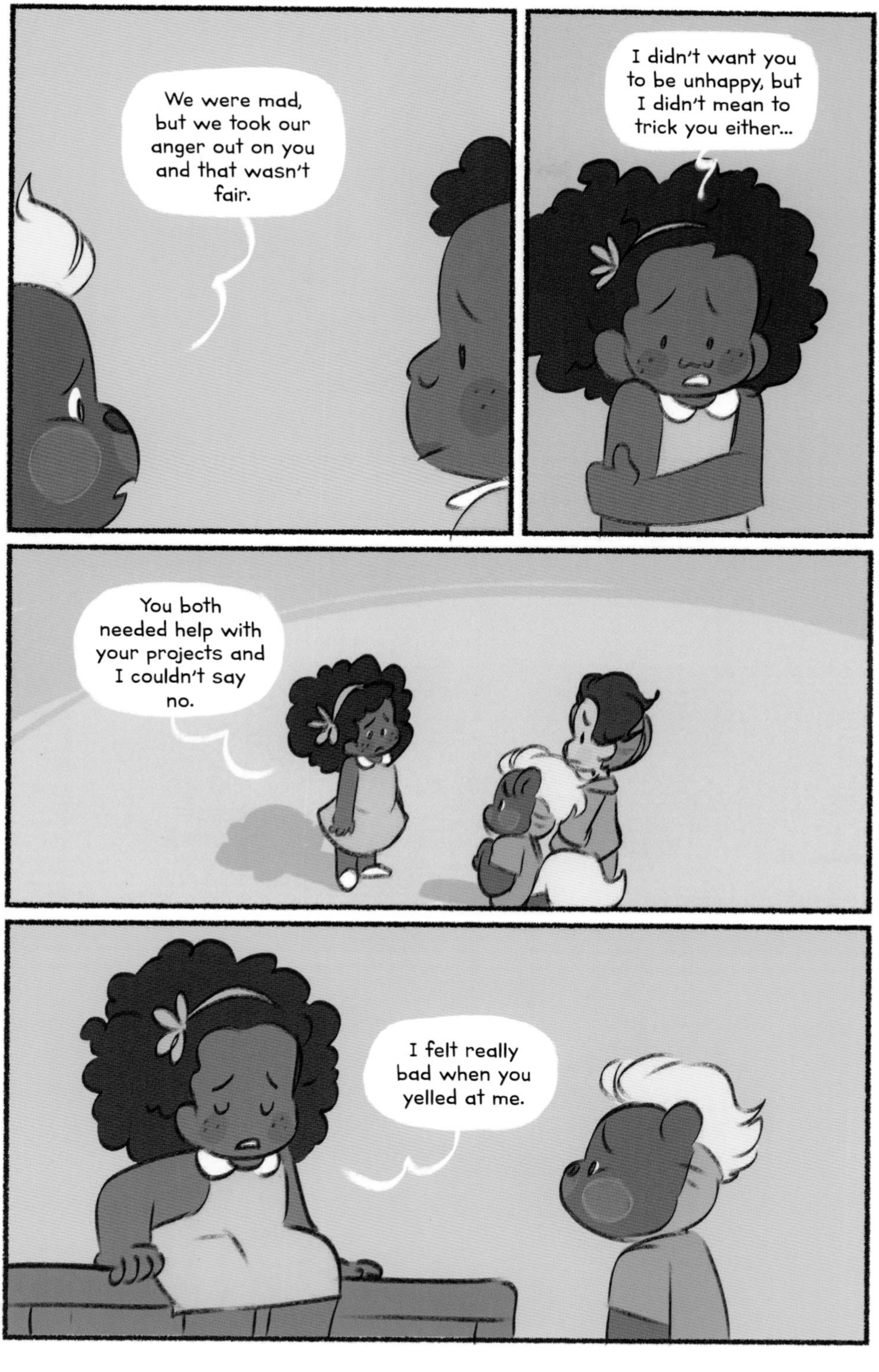

We were mad, but we took our anger out on you and that wasn't fair.
I didn't want you to be unhappy, but I didn't mean to trick you either...
You both needed help with your projects and I couldn't say no.
I felt really bad when you yelled at me.

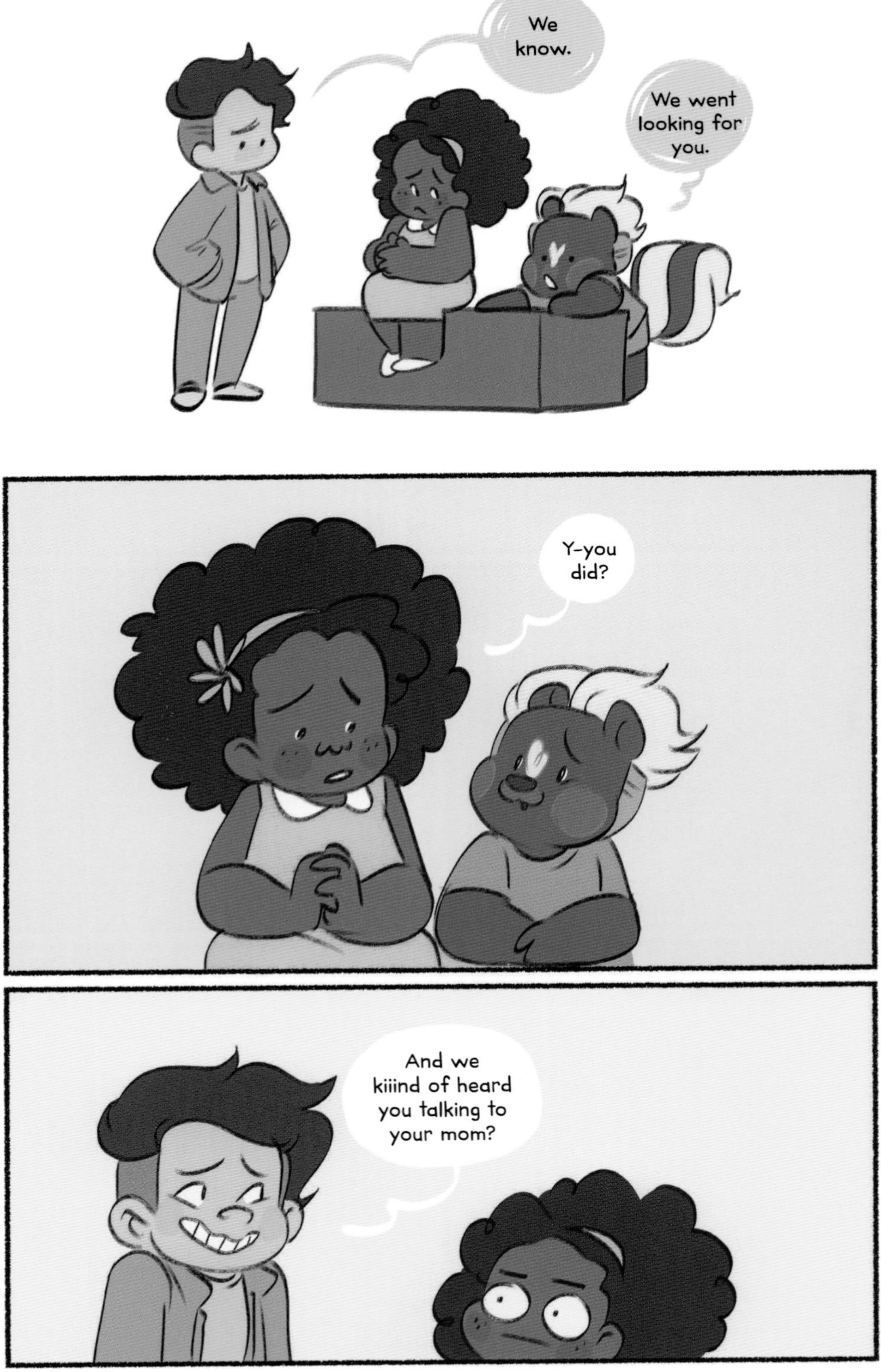
We know.
We went looking for you.
Y-you did?
And we kiiind of heard you talking to your mom?

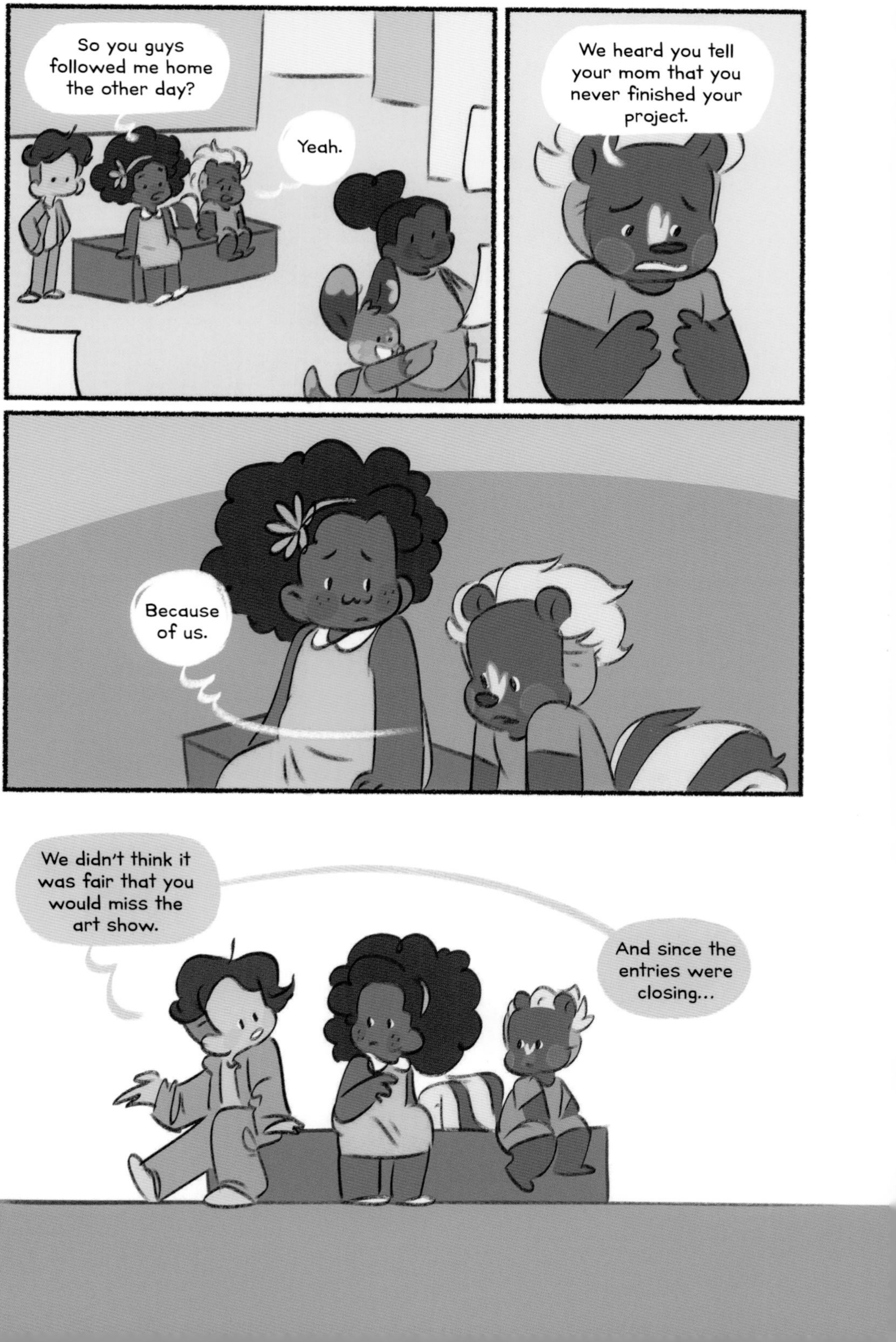
So you guys followed me home the other day?
Yeah.
We heard you tell your mom that you never finished your project.
Because of us.
We didn't think it was fair that you would miss the art show.
And since the entries were closing...

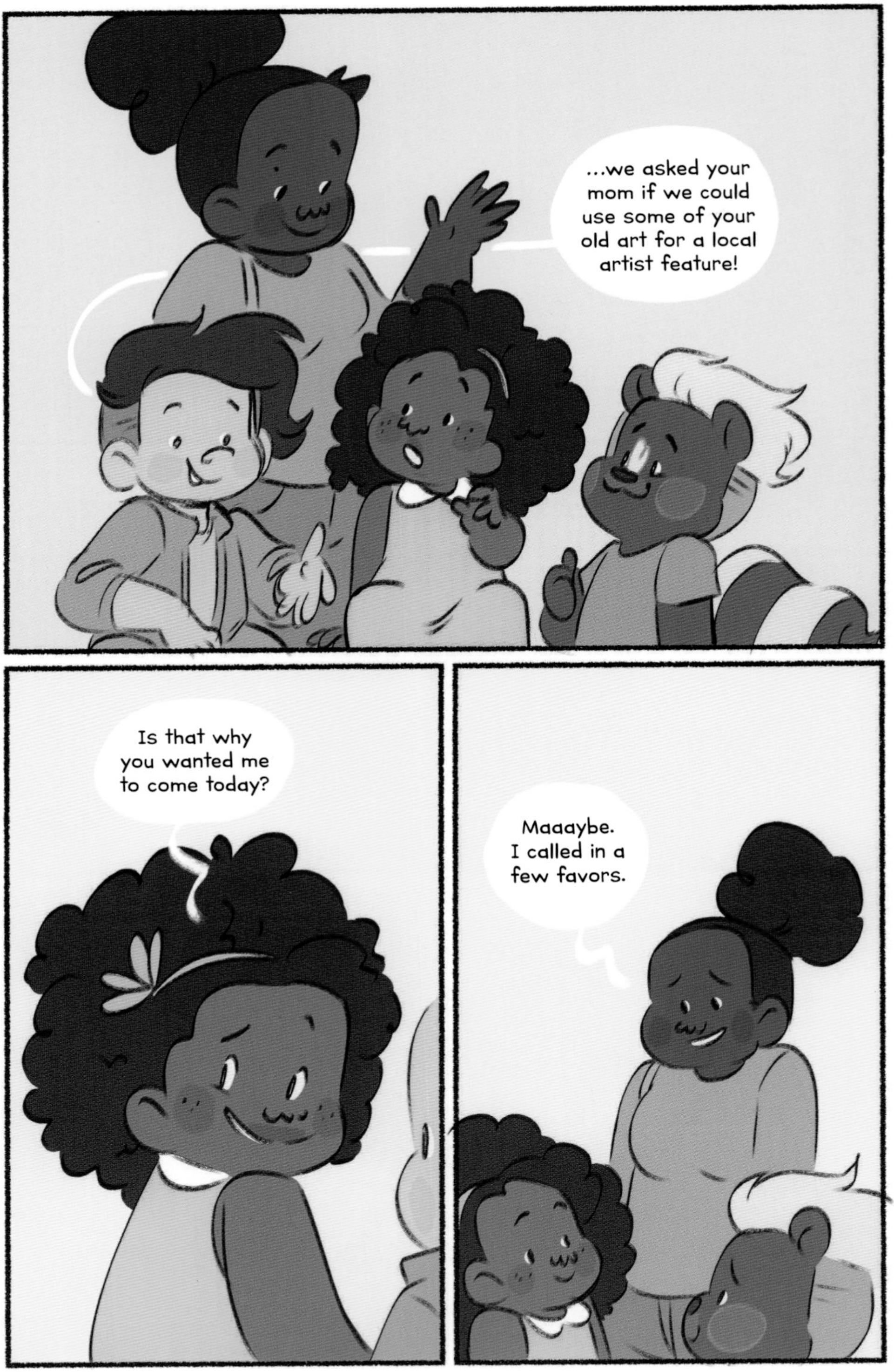
...we asked your mom if we could use some of your old art for a local artist feature!
Is that why you wanted me to come today?
Maaaybe. I called in a few favors.

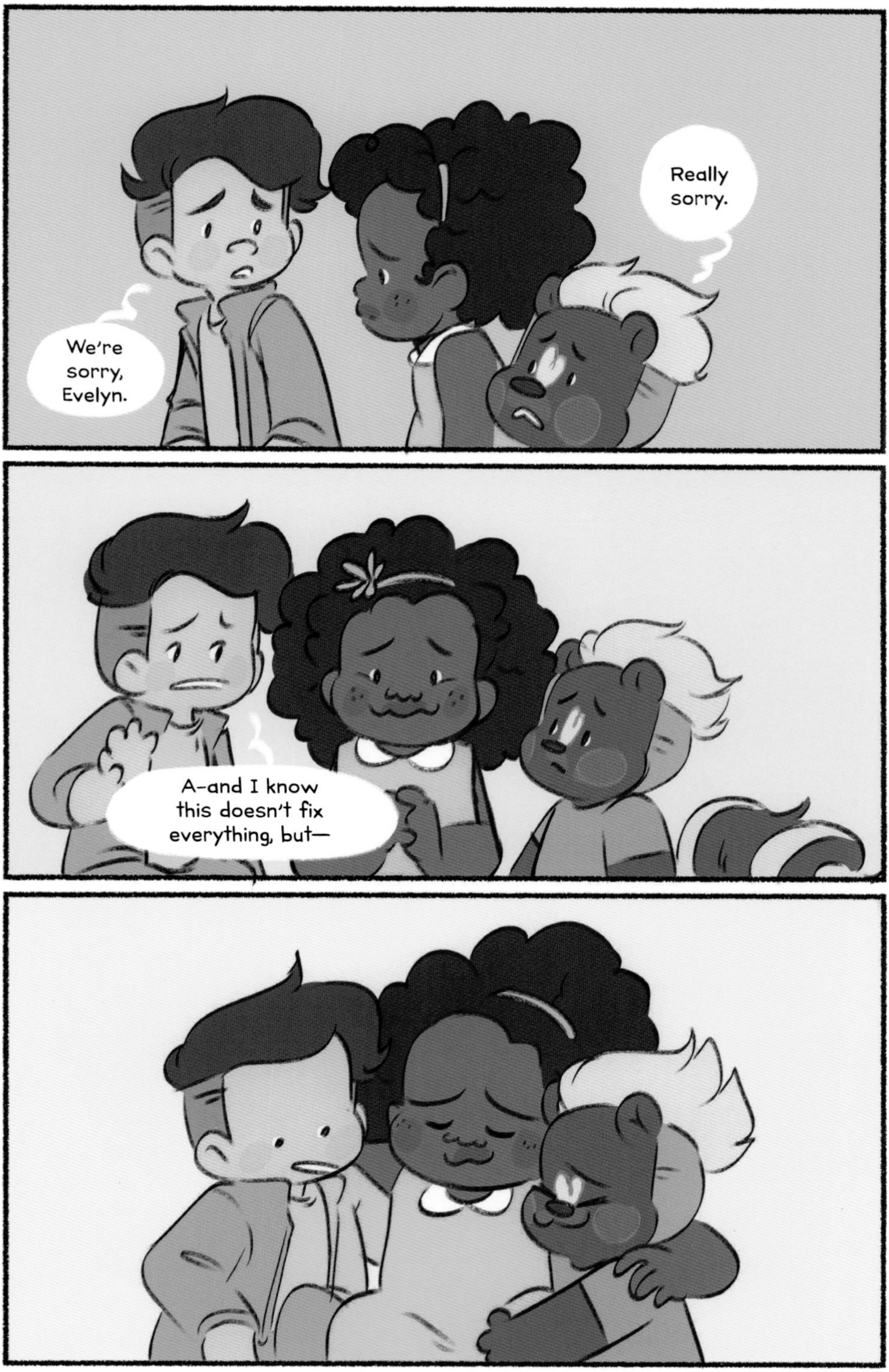
We're sorry, Evelyn.
Really sorry.
A-and I know this doesn't fix everything, but—

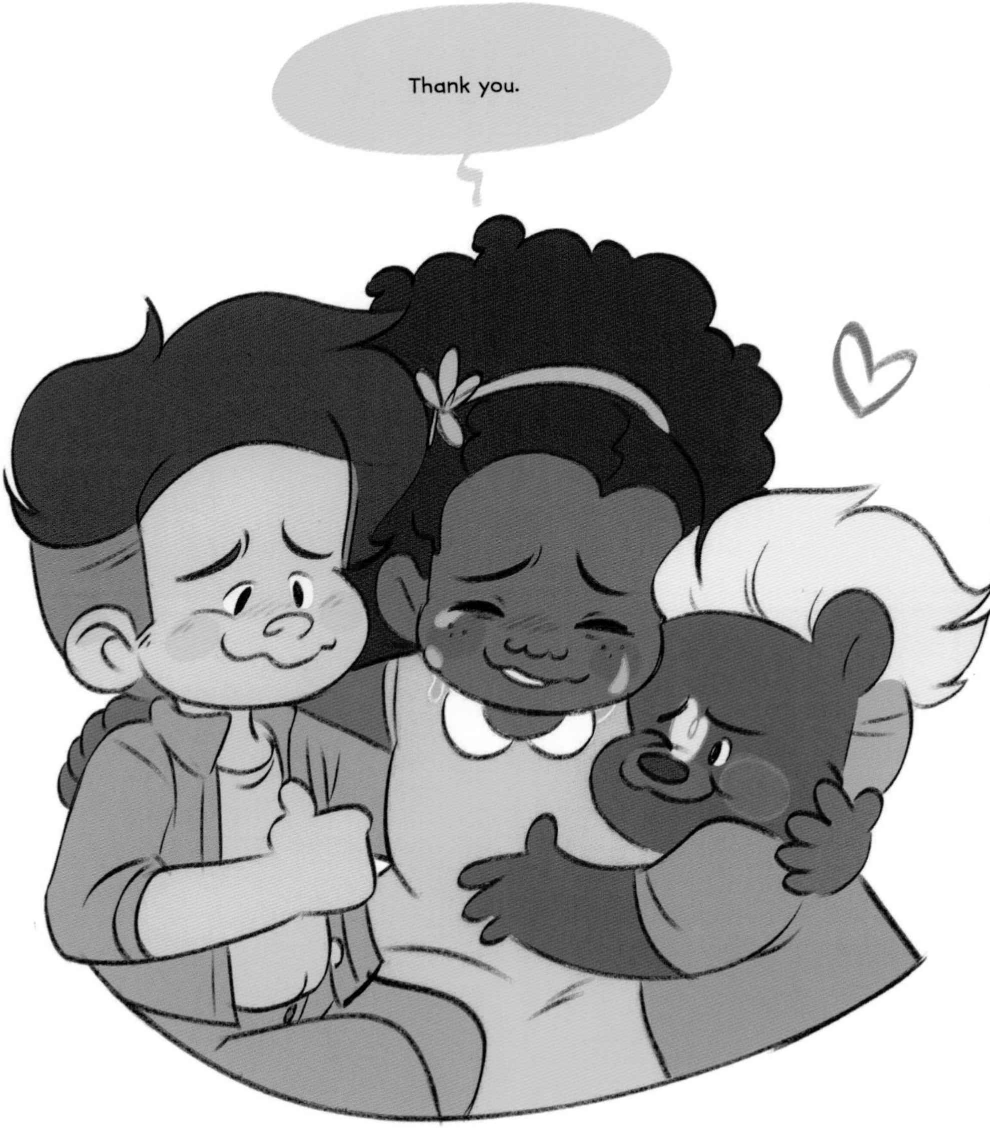
Thank you.

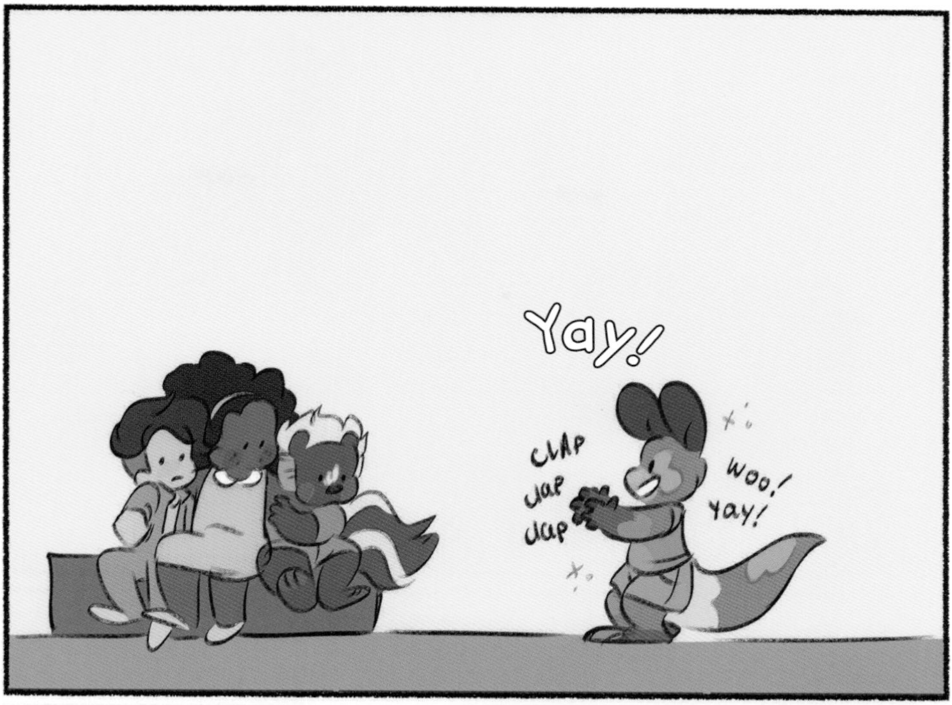
Yay!
CLAP
clap
clap
woo!
yay!

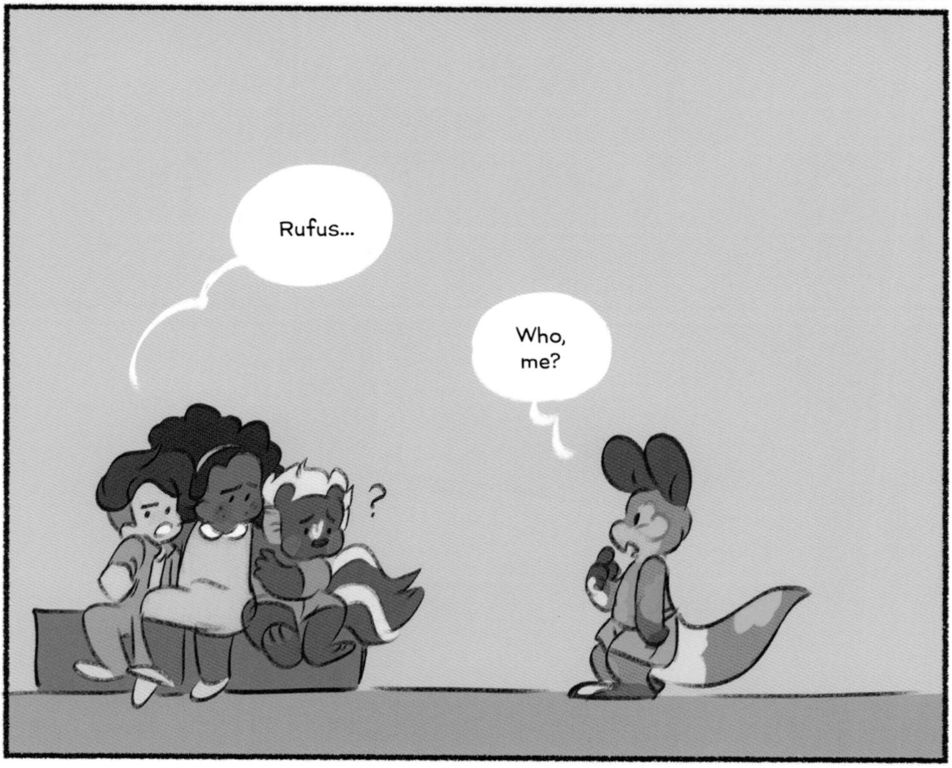
Rufus...
Who,
me?
?

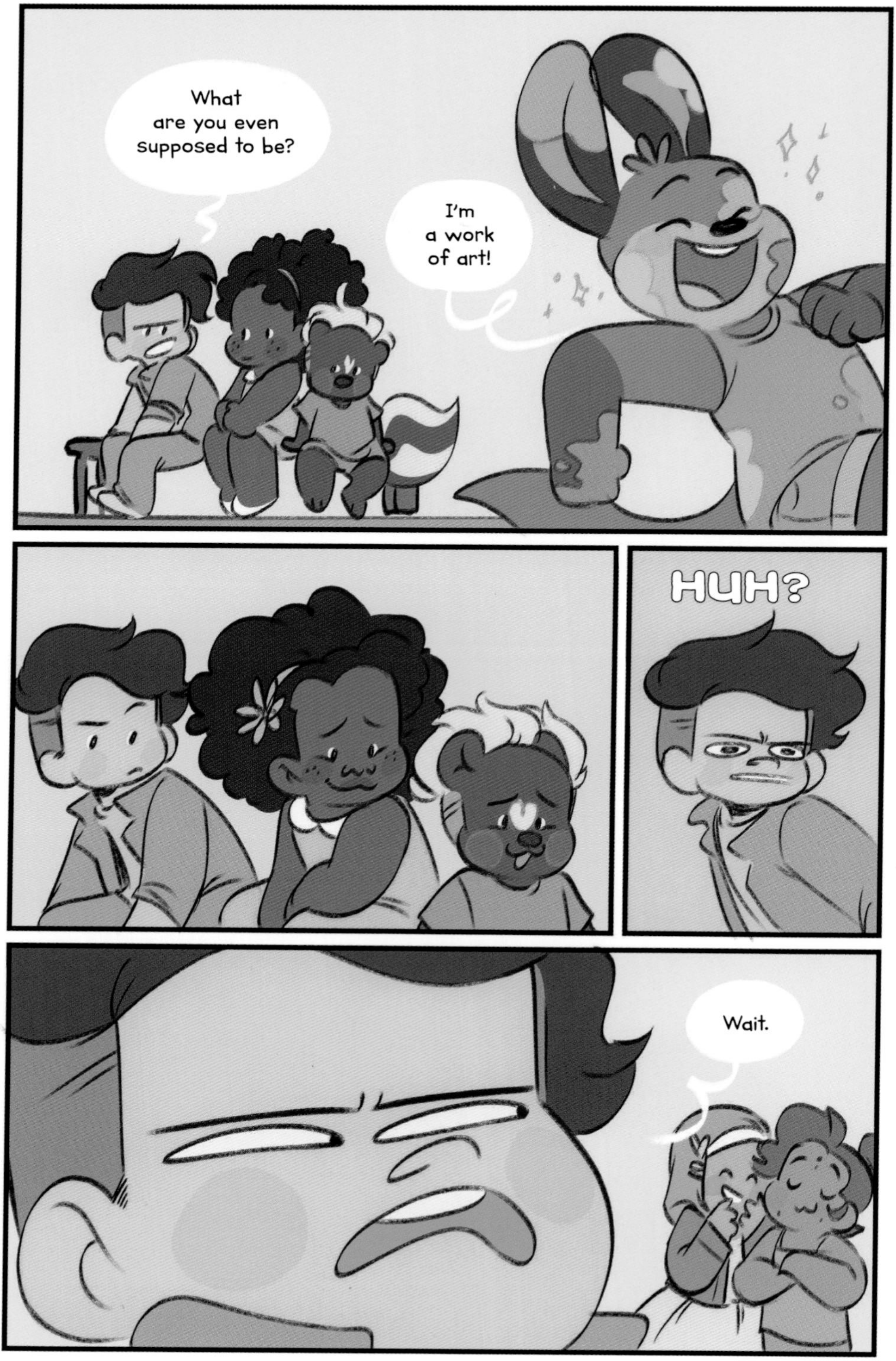
What are you even supposed to be?
I'm a work of art!
HUH?
Wait.

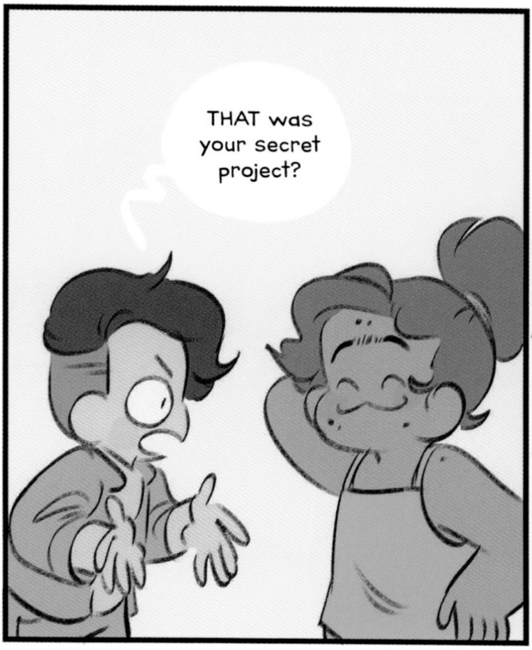
THAT was your secret project?

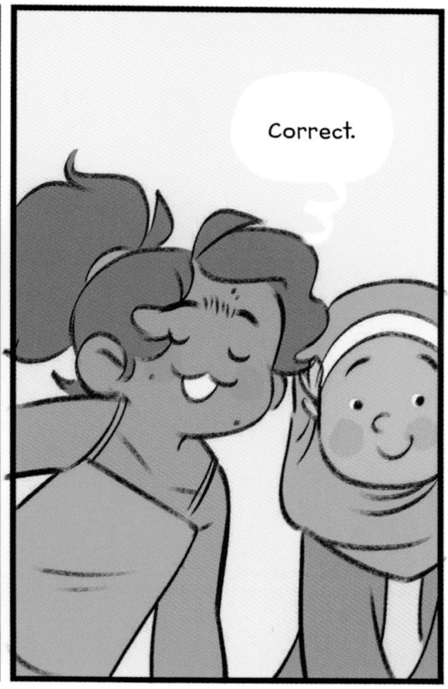
Correct.

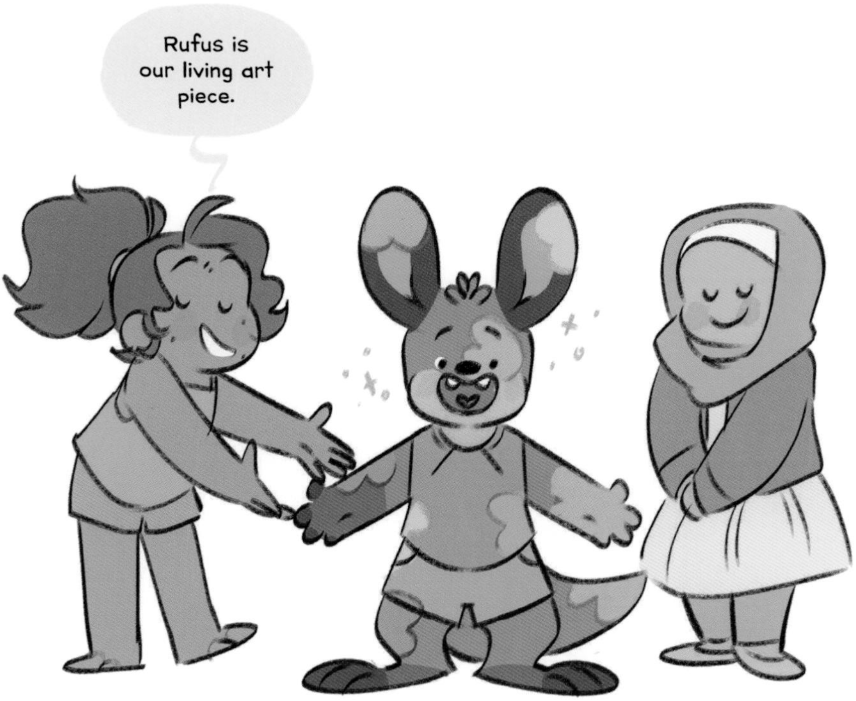
Rufus is our living art piece.

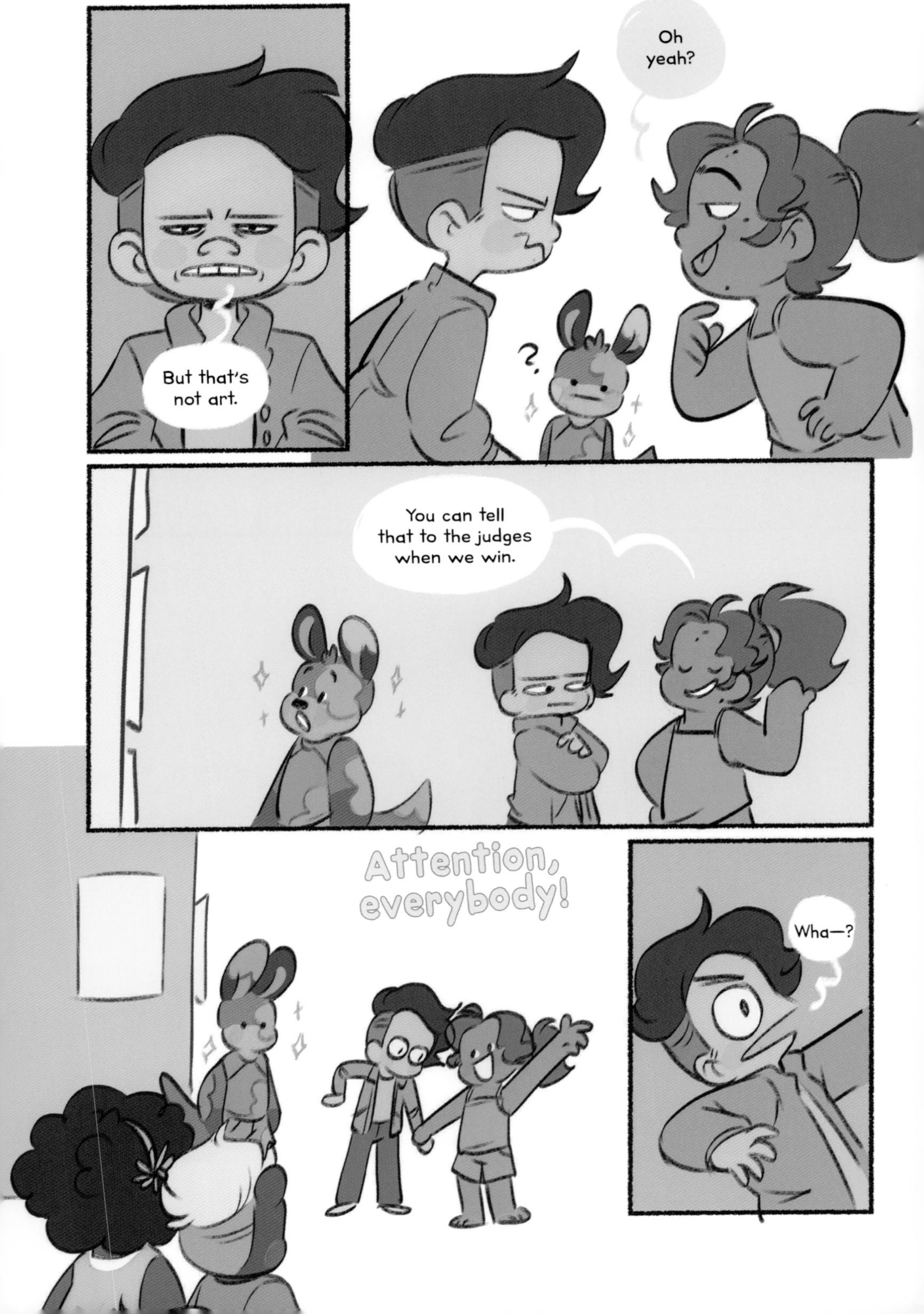
But that's not art.
Oh yeah?
?
You can tell that to the judges when we win.
Attention, everybody!
Wha—?

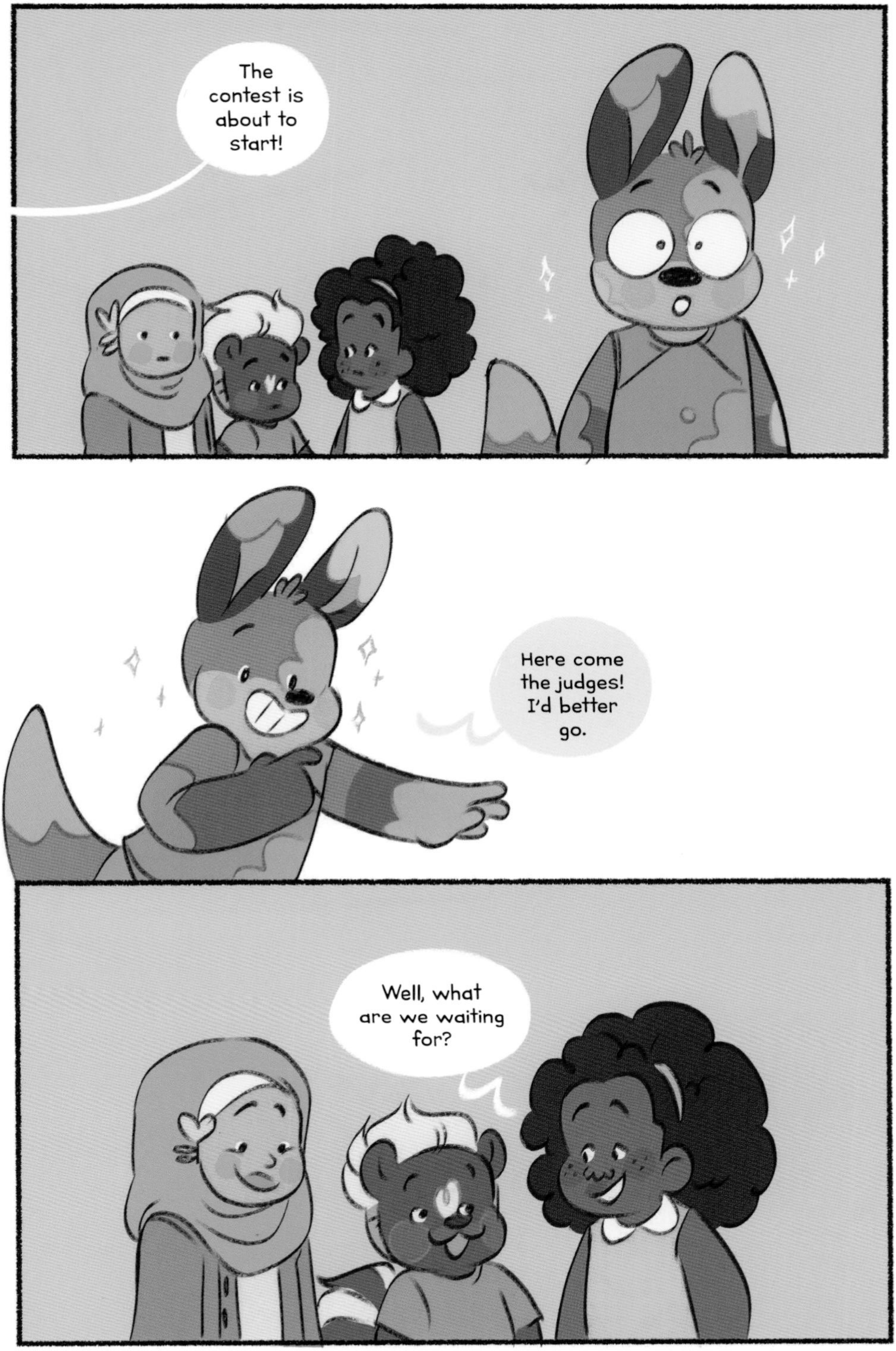
The contest is about to start!
Here come the judges! I'd better go.
Well, what are we waiting for?

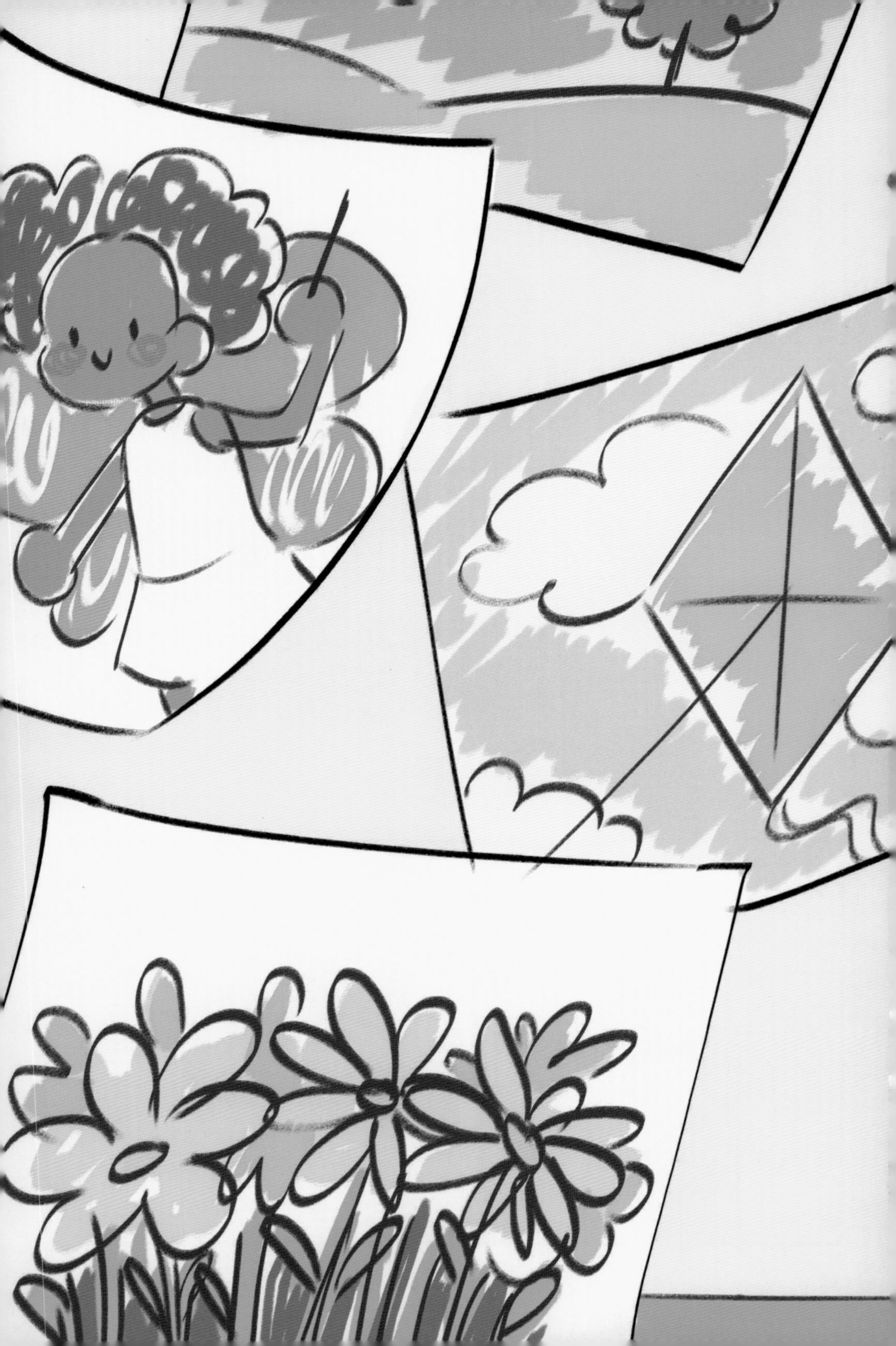

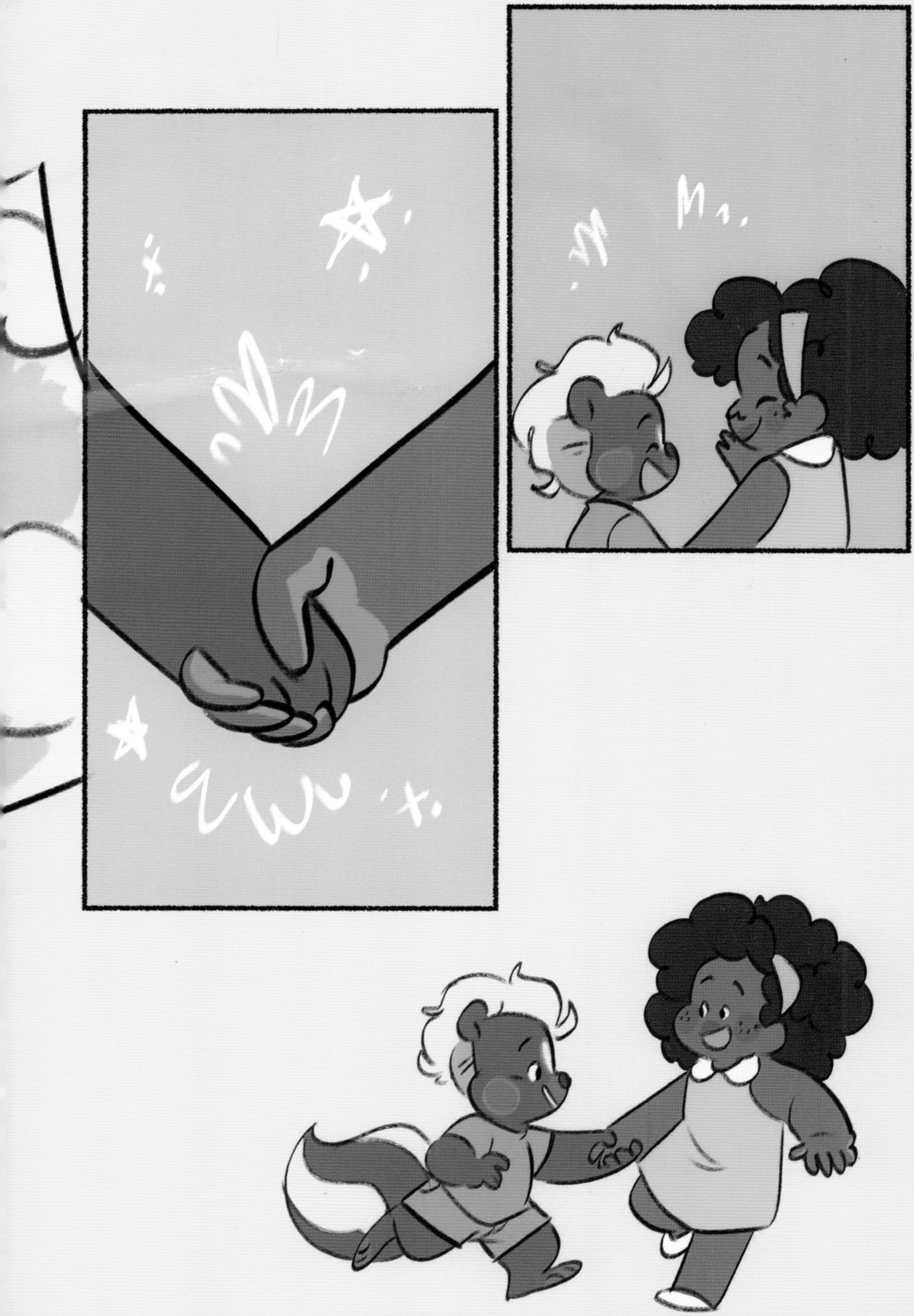

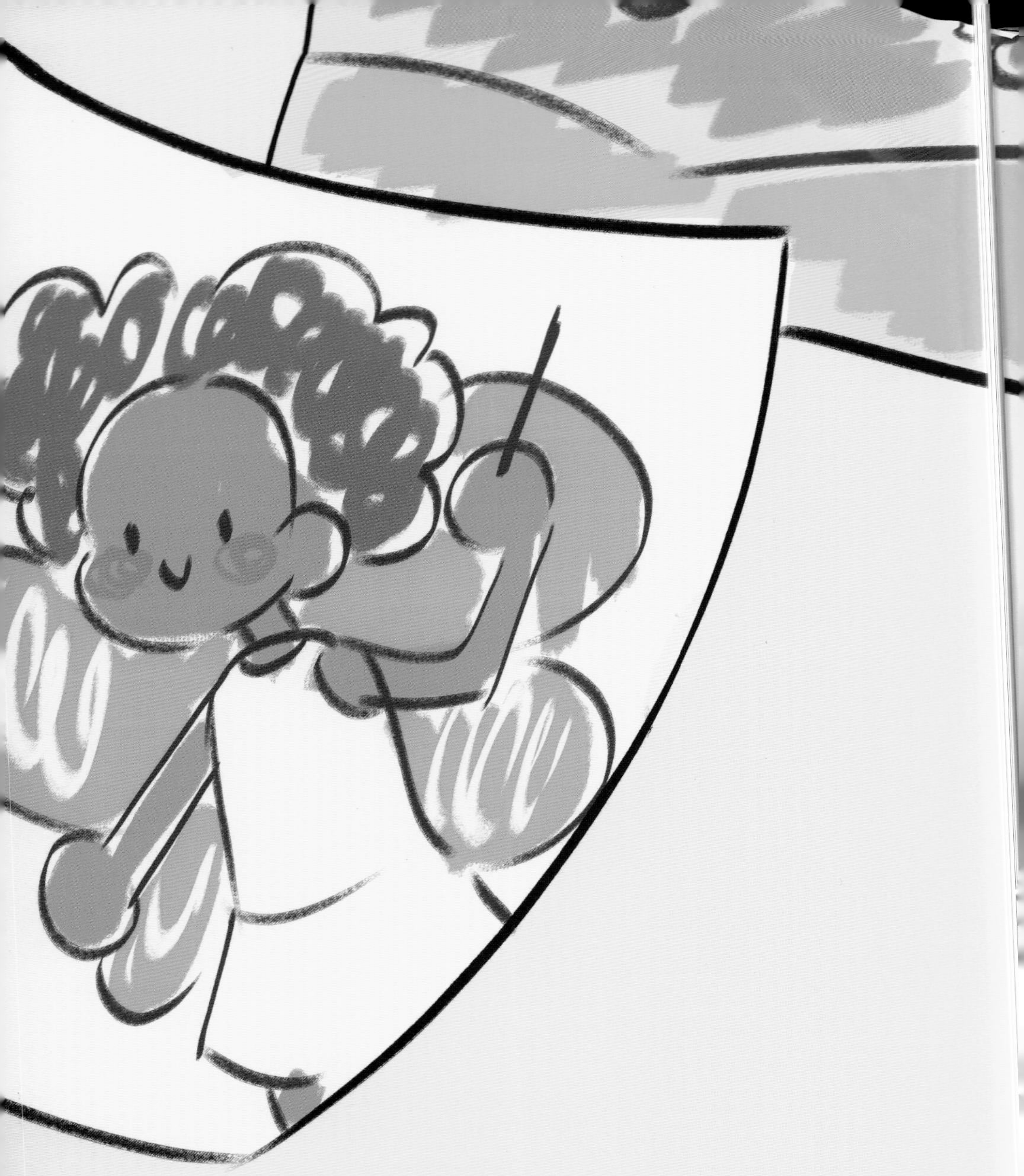

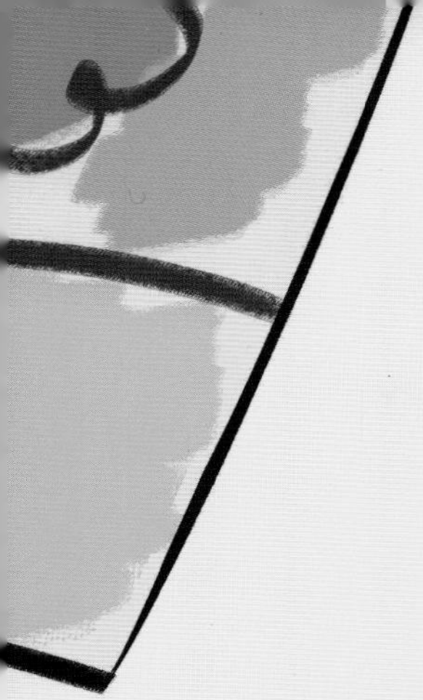

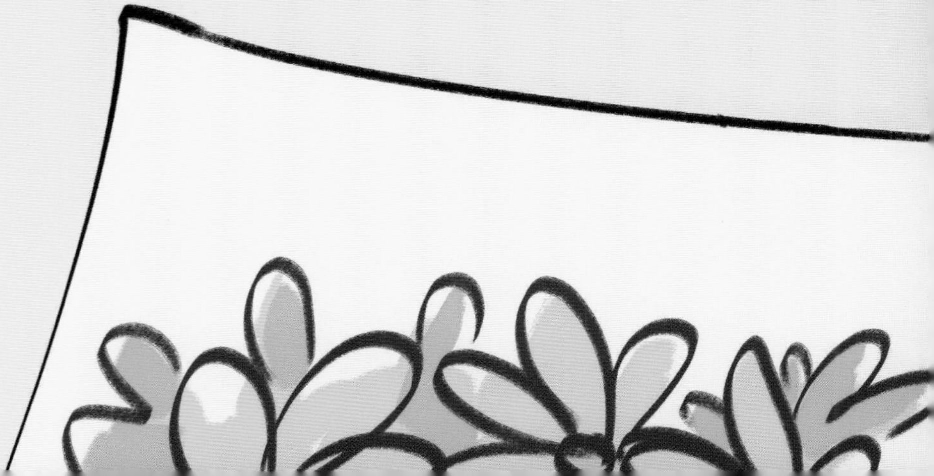

ACKNOWLEDGMENTS

A lot of love went into the making of this book, but I'd like to personally thank . . .

Britt Siess, for your wisdom, advocacy, and guidance through this funny thing called publishing! I couldn't ask for a better agent.

Kait Feldmann and Bones Leopard, for seeing Evelyn and Avery's potential from the beginning. I am forever grateful. (Did you spot your cameos yet?)

Gale Galligan, Shannon Wright, Chad Sell, and Caytlin Vilbrandt, for giving me opportunities to grow as a cartoonist.

Anya Samukova and Cindy Harris, for being excellent in every way.

And finally, my family and friends, who have encouraged and supported me over the years. I love you all.

ELLE ♡
PIERRE